Please feel free to send me an email. Just kr
these emails. Good news is always welcom(

Hollie Armstrong - hollie_armstrong@awesomeauthors.org

Sign up for my blog for updates and freebies!
hollie-armstrong.awesomeauthors.org

About the Publisher

BLVNP Incorporated, A Nevada Corporation, 340 S. Lemon #6200, Walnut CA 91789, info@blvnp.com / legal@blvnp.com

The Best Part of Hello

By: Hollie Armstrong

BLVNP

ISBN: 978-1-64434-023-3

Table of Contents

FREE DOWNLOAD

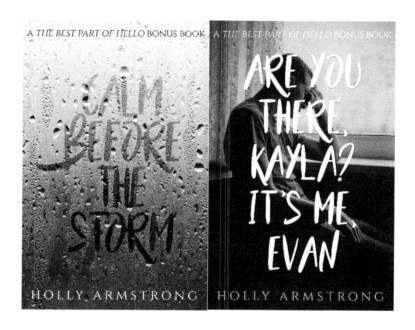

Get these freebies and MORE when you sign up
for the author's mailing list!

hollie-armstrong.awesomeauthors.org

Chapter One

Lately, I have been thinking a lot about choices.

Not the ones I make, but the choices people around me seem to be making. For instance, why Susy Donovan thinks it is okay to pick her toenails on this plane journey to Italy, her bare feet on the seat as her nail clippers snap the ends of her toenails off. But more importantly, why Evan Winters believes my armrest is his pillow.

"You're doing it again," I moan over the loud rumble of turbulence that throws me against the window. My book falls from my hands and lands next to Evan, who has propped his jacket up on the armrest and is lying awkwardly on it, his long legs tucked under the seat, rather than in front. He doesn't bother replying but makes a point of adjusting his position and closing his eyes. It's early morning, and I know I should be asleep, but between the turbulence and Evan's tickly coat, it's pretty much impossible.

"*Hello*, move your coat to the other side," I say again, flicking the top of Evan's forehead. His immediate reaction is to tense up, and he opens one eye, looking up at me, but he's upside down. I'm leaning over him, so his face looks funny. His eyes are wonky from this position, and his nose sticks out so far, I can see inside his nostrils, it's pretty gross. But the more I look, the more I notice all his other features. He's got full lips, the type of ones that people with fillers would be jealous over and a thick band of eyelashes that makes *me* jealous.

"I can't move it there," he replies gruffly, opening the other eye.

"And why ever not?"

"Because that side gives me a headache. I can't lie like that without waking up with a dodgy neck," he complains.

"Your neck will be the least of your worries if you don't move," I threaten, though it's weak and holds little meaning to it; I know I couldn't even punch my way out of a paper bag.

Evan begins laughing, and I can tell in his eyes he's recounting the experience himself. "Do you remember…God, when was it? Fifth grade? When you tried punching your way out of a paper bag?" He chuckles. Susy Donovan, who until this very second has been very intent on her toenails, looks over at the two of us and frowns as if we are the problem here.

"I did no such thing," I lie, but I'm trying to stifle a giggle. "I have no idea what you're talking about."

"Oh, own up to it." Evan snorts. "I remember it. You were standing on your front porch with that grocery bag and who was it—"

"Toby Rhinestone," we both say together.

"Yeah," he carries on. "Toby told you that your muscles were as weak as a floppy fish because you couldn't carry those two bags in. I remember you trying to punch the inside of this bag, and all you did was dent it a bit." Evan laughs again, looking at me quizzically. "I mean it was made of paper, Kayla."

"Shut up." I nudge him off my armrest. "I wasn't exactly trying to prove a point."

"Whatever you say." He holds his hands up and moves his coat. "But try avoiding the physical threats when you know the only thing you can damage is the inside of a paper bag."

"You never stop talking, do you?" It comes out more like a question rather than a statement. I see Evan hold his grin, an expression of sheer amusement laced over every feature of his face. Since he is sitting up, his hair has gone matted and seems a darker shade of brown in this light. He tries fixing it in the reflection on the plane window, but it gets him nowhere.

"Not when I'm right," he says after a moment.

I roll my eyes. "So, where's Jess?"

I flip open the tray compartment on the back of the chair and pick up my book from the floor. Evan doesn't look my way as I refer to his girlfriend, so I press further.

"Let me guess." I entertain myself, holding my hands out in front of me. "No comment here, folks." I snigger to myself. Evan doesn't talk about things like this. He doesn't really talk much at all, not usually. He's the silent and broody type, always the one in the corner who keeps to himself. He's got a small circle of friends, and they don't interact with anyone else but themselves. If they aren't speaking in low voices in class to each other, they are behind the bike shed with a cigarette dangling out of their mouths.

"You're so weird," he mutters and rotates his cell phone in his palms aimlessly. He can't use it, but there seems to be a dire need to ever since we got on the plane hours earlier. He has been holding it even as he was sleeping.

"Where is she?" I ask again. "I thought you two were like *super* close." I peek out of the corner of my eye for his reaction, but he's sitting up straight, and his expression is stone cold. The grin that once was there has vanished.

He turns to look at me this time, a tendril of brown hair escaping from his matted mane. "Don't sit here and pretend to know who I am and what I do," he says defensively. His complete change of attitude confuses me.

"I don't pretend. I'm not a child, Evan, and I can tell that you two practically kiss the shit out of each other's asses," I retort. He's doing it again, stirring the angry side of me. We've been at each other's throats for as long as I can remember; it's like an unspoken rule between us: we just don't get along. I guess this is why I flipped when Mrs. Scott, our leader and teacher for this trip, told me I was to be plane partners with my next-door neighbor. My reaction told her I wasn't happy, and she made a point of saying it wasn't personal, and that everyone was matched by their last names. She said they paired the first in the alphabet with the last until they met in the middle and considering my surname is Burns and Evan's is Winters, we fell exactly where I didn't want to be.

"Oh, like you and bony little Benjamin over there?" He fires back with force. "I'm over a hundred percent sure he's gay."

My mouth widens, and I make a face. "Are you seriously lowering yourself to think that someone's sexuality is an insult?" I quip. "I will have you know that everyone in this world is equal and despite your clearly pea-sized brain, that includes you too—"

"Look, Kayla," he interrupts, "I don't want to hear a lecture on all your feminism bullshit. I'm tired and uncomfortable, and I'm sitting on a ten-hour flight with one of the loudest and most talkative girls I have ever met, so shut it will you because I'm about to pass out from all the crap you're babbling into my ear."

"Fifty-eight."

"What?" he asks, irritated.

I grin, the sarcasm thick in my words. "You just spoke fifty-eight words to me in that rant. I think that's a record."

"Get a life."

And even as the plane descends, and we are being led into the brisk night air of Rome, Italy where we will be spending the next two weeks, I don't utter another word. I occasionally giggle, every time Evan meets my eye. Sophie, my best friend, who is also British which means everything that comes out of her mouth is basically magic to my ears, catches up with me and gushes about a story from her flight with Jack Watson.

"I'm sorry for ditching you," she finishes. "How were things down your end?"

I give her a look as if to say, 'don't ask,' but still relay the last ten hours to her in vivid detail.

.   .   .

And somehow, we end up here.

Enclosed between five walls and a packet of chips between us, my senior class is sitting on their luggage, mouths quite literally falling to their chins and a stare that could make someone turn to stone. I seemed to be the only vocal student out of the pack after the journey we have had.

"You have *got* to be kidding me," I toss my hands over my head for emphasis and point to the dungeon that we have been trapped in. The whitewashed walls that give no signs of life suddenly make me what to scream. "This trip was supposed to be fun, *explore our creative minds* or whatever." A flash of anger flutters over my eyes, and I look back and see my suitcase has fallen over which only adds a dramatic flair.

Mrs. Scott, our teacher, shakes her head. She's an older woman, mid-fifties, who constantly wears a pencil skirt that is made from a sort of hard-wearing material. Her blond bob shakes as she speaks. "Kayla, we're all upset, but there is nothing I can do. The storm is—" but she doesn't get to finish because someone else's voice cuts through.

"Yes, the storm is horrendous. Torrential rain, it's not safe, etc., etc. We get your point. But what we all want to know is: when is the next plane out of this dump?" Evan Winters steps out of the shadows, quite prominently making himself known. His usual brood is in the corner, eyeing him carefully. I see his best friends sitting on their luggage, waiting expectantly for what Evan will say next, and it isn't just those two who are staring. Evan's barely mouthed a word to any of us in the last five years of school; it's kind of a phenomenon to see he's got one.

But what Evan says next isn't wonderfully scripted or helpful in the slightest. It is once again focused on the only person Evan Winters remotely cares for: himself. "There has got to be a vending machine in here right?"

"Are you joking?" I cry. And here's round two of Kayla, aka myself, losing it over something Evan Winters says or does. "We are quite literally stranded in an airport in a country that none of us speaks the native language of, and you," I frown considerably, "are thinking about your freaking stomach?"

"That's enough from you, Miss Burns," Mrs. Scott warns, and she raises her eyebrows at Evan. "We are all going to have to try and make the best of this situation." But she too flops onto a waiting room chair just as it happens. An alarm strikes.

"What's happening?" Sophie calls out as we all jump up from our suitcases. The alarm is loud and rings in my ears so much that I can't hear the yelps of fright coming from my classmates. I feel somebody grab the palm of my hand and it's Ben, my boyfriend. He's saying something I can't hear, and I just shake my head, gesturing towards my ears. He only nods, moving so that I am stepping in time with the other students who seem to be heading towards the windows to see what is going on.

It's like watching a movie. All the windows and doors are automatically shutting and I see crowds of people being ushered inside another building by security men. Some of the security men near us instruct something in Italian and point towards another room across the waiting room. We all go running as the grumble of the storm outside picks up, and the students around me shriek with shock. I am clutching onto Ben so hard that my fingers are numb.

"We're going into lockdown," I hear one of the students say. I think I recognize him from my Biology class. "I've seen this on documentaries. It's something airports and other large public places do when there's either an outbreak of some disease or in this case, a dangerous circumstance." He gets a few puzzled looks. "The storm?" He sighs.

Ben and I look at each other worriedly and escape down the staircase. It's mayhem, people pushing into me and stumbling down the stairs. Security guards try and direct us, but the language barrier is complicated and only makes things worse. We are directed to a small panic room that has no windows and only one door—the one we came through. As we all file in, our teachers try and direct us in an organized manner, but the panicked looks on their faces only tell me that they are out of control too.

The last couple of students file into the room, both crying as the guards make a move to lock and secure the door. I'm squeezing Ben's hand so much that he turns to look at me.

"You alright babe?" He swings an arm around my waist and pulls me close. I nod into his chest and look over his shoulder. He's tall, and I have to go on my tip toes.

"I have no idea what's going on. It was fine when we arrived," I say, referring to the weather. Stepping off the plane it was cold, brisk, maybe a little windy but nothing to this extent. It's like the weather did a 180 in the space of an hour.

I watch our suitcases being tossed into the corner of the room by a group of security men and I walk over to try and retrieve mine. The number of guards seems to have doubled, the sound of their radios buzzing around the room.

"They're saying it's a freak storm," Ben explains. I didn't realize he had followed. "My Italian is a little rusty, but it looks like the airport is on lockdown." He grabs my case for me.

"I already feel like I could kill someone," I exaggerate. "I haven't slept or eaten anything properly in eleven hours." I fight the urge to complain more.

Ben laughs, kissing the top of my head. "Just remember babe," he tightens his grip. "There's no Netflix in prison." I smile, despite everything. But it drops the moment I hear it: the rumble of the storm and a pain-filled scream, but as quickly as it comes, it's gone.

Chapter Two

It hasn't stopped, the rumble of the storm is brewing like a bubbling kettle that is about to explode. The noise engulfs the small room we are all huddled in—along with the complaints from everyone who is starving.

"How long do you think we're going to have to wait here?" Sophie's got a pair of sweats thrown over her shoulder as she desperately tries to root through her luggage for a hairbrush. She's as impatient as ever and flings a pair of shorts in my direction which I almost don't catch. "My stomach literally feels as if it's going to fall out my arse," she adds sarcastically, even her way of pronouncing 'ass' isn't enough to make me smile.

I disregard her comment with a frown, despite feeling the same. Soph could be vulgar sometimes, but it was kind of the best thing about her. She always spoke her mind no matter what was on it. I guess in some situations it just wasn't appropriate.

I shrug my shoulders and sigh in a long, heavy breath and finally respond to her. "When the storm blows over, probably. I mean, it's likely going to be over in the morning." I try reassuring her, though, by the looks of it, the worst is yet to come.

"Gather round!" Mrs. Scott whistles, her fingers pressed to her lips. "I have news."

Sophie and I stand, joining the crowd of teenagers that are moving towards her. I look for Ben, but he's not back yet. He had gone with another teacher and a few other students in search of a food source over an hour ago.

I can't help but question this airport. Aren't they supposed to have rations when things like this occur? Protocols and procedures? The security guards haven't so much as been in this room since we were pushed in here and I haven't seen any airport staff since we landed. I'm so consumed by thoughts that I don't notice another flash of lighting glaring through the room, followed by a large clap of thunder that makes everyone shriek and jumps. I jump too, my spiral of thoughts evaporating, and clutch onto Sophie's hand, my heart racing. I've never seen thunder like this before. It was like watching a movie, except I was in it.

Mrs. Scott and the rest of the teachers do their best to calm us, but the wind is howling, making its presence known, and Mrs. Scott's voice is small as she tries to compete with the roaring terrain outside.

"I'm going to have to shout," she yells. "But as you might have known, some of our teachers have gone to find a vending machine or another food source at this airport. I know that this place is huge, but due to safety precautions, this part of the airport is being blocked off from terminals A and B, which hold the rest of the passengers. I am also aware that this experience isn't the one that was planned, however, there is no point sitting here dwelling on it.

"It's our job now to work together and get through this storm as best we can. This means communication and cooperation are essential. I want you all to pair up and use the blankets that the security have found to create a bed on the floor here. It's going to be a squeeze and you're going to have to make a pillow from a ball of clothes, but it's imperative that now you follow through and make sure that you know where you're sleeping and that it's reasonable—if not somewhat comfortable."

She dips her head slightly. "This is definitely not ideal, and I apologize that we have been stranded in this situation. I cannot control the weather, though I am praying the clouds will give way and we can get out of here. So, grab a partner and get moving. I will be leaving shortly to help with the food finding."

And briskly after she leaves, we all separate from each other, orderly digging out a blanket from the stack at the door and get to work. Mrs. Scott is right. We must stick together. We don't have anything else.

• • •

It's 10:50 European time when Ben and the others return from their search for food. Most of our senior class is trying to settle down, heads on pillows and eyes closed. Nobody is asleep. It's the thunder that keeps everyone awake.

Ben walks into the center, stepping over a couple of students on his path. I watch him produce a packet of cookies, a large tub of something orange and a collection of spoons. It's not much, but it's something. My stomach rumbles as if on cue.

"Dinner!" he announces. A bunch of us shot up in hopes to see something meal-like in front of us, but instead, we are disappointed.

"We found a tub of cold carrot and coriander soup in the staff room along with these funky looking cookies," he explains. "There's only twenty spoons here so tough luck. Share. It's not going to be the spreading of germs that will kill you." Ben chuckles along with some others.

A group of seniors stand and walk towards the middle and pick two of the spoons up and take some of the soup from the tub. Four spoonfuls down, they hand over the spoons to their friends, who wipe the spoon with kitchen roll and proceed to do the same. I look around the room, my eyes scanning over to Evan and his clan in the far corner. There's sixty-eight of us and only twenty spoons and a pack of ten cookies.

This has got to be a joke.

"What kind of airport isn't prepared for this sort of stuff?" I question Sophie, who only meagerly shrugs like she never heard me in the first place. Sophie and I are the last to get our share, and the soup is bitter and cold, but I swallow it down anyway. I'm ravenous. Ben had split the cookies up into halves and gave them to the teachers to munch on as they could only manage a small spoonful of soup between them. *It's ridiculous*, I tell myself, *but it can only be for one night*. I try and think of the breakfast I'll have tomorrow, but it only makes my stomach churn for more.

I don't fall asleep until around one in the morning. But by the time I have, I am being woken up by the sound of footsteps. It's pitch black when my eyes fly open, but a man walks past me, brushing the edge of his jeans on my arm. At first, I'm convinced it's Ben. Who else would be getting up and walking over to me in the early morning? But my guess is wrong, and as the door edges open, someone slips out of it.

I throw the blanket off me and slip on some shoes. I don't know what compels me to do this because everything I have ever told myself is that you don't follow someone out of a door and into the dark, especially in a situation like this. But I find myself leaning down to tie my laces. I hear Sophie turning in her sleep, and I freeze, careful not to wake her anymore. Once I'm convinced she's sleeping, I follow the man out of the room.

I'm surprised to see it's not dark outside of the door. All of the lights illuminate how much glass is now littering the floor, a broken window allowing space for wind to blow through. It's freezing, so much so that I think about going back to get a jacket, but something out of the corner of my eye catches my attention—a figure moving. I push myself to continue and not turn back.

"Right," I say to nothing and nobody. A check-in desk is across the room from me, the door behind hanging off its hinges. I know I saw the figure go through there. The sound of the wind crashing against the windows makes me jump. I can feel the cold start to tickle at my bare skin. I know it's now or never.

I go as far as trying to mentally pump myself up even though I know this is insane. *I can do this*, I tell myself, and I do. I begin running towards the opposite end of the check-in desk and I only just make it before I can hear the storm starting up again. A hurling wind rips through the window and a wooden plank presumably picked up from outside is thrown to the ground.

"Holy shit," I whisper, shaking in fright.

I spin around and pull the door slightly which illuminates a dark corridor. It's one of those moments I know I shouldn't follow through with, but I can't help myself, I begin to walk. The eerie quietness unsettles me as I look from left to right down the corridor. It's made up of rooms on each side, completely parallel to each other. Suitcases sit on tables and computers and files decorate the desks of the rooms I can see into. I assume this is where security takes you to be interviewed if they believe you are a possible risk to the plane or national security or something. It looks like one of the rooms out of a TV show I binge watch at home.

I'm too busy looking through one of the windows into a room when I notice a light flickering like crazy. I trip over my own two feet, crashing into the wall and curse loudly as my funny bone makes contact with the wall. A bang signals from the end of the corridor, but I have no time to think about it because someone is throwing their arm over my mouth and pulling me back into a room on the opposite side of the corridor. I thrash about, entering the pitch black and struggle to get free. I can feel the wind brushing my feet, but the hand is strong over my mouth, so I decide to bite it.

"Fuck!" My kidnapper lets go and I back into the table, wildly looking towards the figure beside the door. I can't see anything, I try to squint, but I'm panicking too much.

"Who are you?" I say, alarmed. I can hear him struggle to find the light switch, but it flickers on. I make eye contact, and I think I want to cry.

"You have *got* to be kidding me," I can feel my wrist ball up against the table. "What the hell do you think you are doing?"

Evan Winters stands with his arms folded and rolls his eyes. "You're *so* dramatic," he says, shaking out his right hand, the one I had bitten.

He moves away from the door and starts talking. "I was finding something substantial to eat," he reaches behind him and produces a packet of Cheetos, "but it looks like you might need them more than I do." He tosses the bag in my direction. They land on the table beside me and a couple spill out.

I pull a face and my stomach rumbles. I don't pick up the packet; there's definitely something more to this. "What are you talking about?"

Evan seems hesitant, but he grabs my hand, pushes me towards the window and points to the end of the corridor. He's forceful, but I notice he is careful not to hurt me which in turn, only makes me confused to what he's trying to show me.

"What am I supposed to be looking at?" The lights aren't bright, and the corridor is still dark, so I can't make out anything.

"Your world," he whispers. And he's right. The more I look, the more I can see two figures at the end of the corridor. I take a step further towards the window, and I see it: the bright blonde hair that I would recognize from anywhere.

My boyfriend is kissing none other than Evan's girlfriend.

Chapter Three

"I'm sorry, can you repeat that?"

Evan and I are staring at each other, mine a more bewildered stare that his look of nonchalance. "This doesn't bother you at all? Or make you angry?" I start to shake my head, pushing back from the window. My head is spinning, and I can't think straight. The image of Ben kissing Jess makes me feel sick. My insides twist at the thought, the image cemented into my brain.

"She's your girlfriend and you don't seem *at all* fazed," I finish, puzzled.

Evan sighs deeply and sits on the edge of a table. "Maybe because she *isn't* my girlfriend,"

"What?" I can feel the anger radiating everywhere. It's loudest in my ears, and I feel myself being consumed by it.

"She's not my girlfriend, Kayla. It's just what everyone thinks, so whatever. She's like my sister." He shrugs but looks up at me for my reaction and takes the bag of chips from the table that I had completely forgotten about.

"Wait, *what?*" This boy confuses me more by the second.

He rolls his eyes again as if this conversation is beneath him and it irks me how relaxed he is. I feel as if my entire universe has gone smashing down on me in a matter of seconds and his lack of emotion infuriates every cell inside my body more. I slap the packet of chips from his hands before he can wolf down the rest.

Evan grunts. "It's not like we kiss or anything. People assume because you're close with a girl then you must be boning her." He takes the bag of chips back.

"But—"

"No buts Kayla, it's pretty simple." He successfully reaches the packet of chips and tips the packet upside down, his mouth catching all the cheesy goodness. My stomach moans at me again, and I curse myself for not stealing a couple when I had the chance.

"You're unbelievable," I say, exasperated.

Evan grins. "Aw, Kayla baby, you're so nice to me."

I make a face. "I just can't believe you didn't make it clear that she wasn't your girlfriend. I mean everyone had pegged you as an idiot because we all knew she was sleeping around with everyone. I thought you were just, you know, an *idiot*." I look at him quizzically before slumping my shoulders.

"But Ben and I…"

"You *were* together." Evan finishes for me. I only nod, not sure what else to say. It is too surreal that I am even talking about this with him.

"There's no need to get upset about it," Evan licks his lips and smiles as if it's just that easy, "he's a complete jerk."

"Yeah," I agree. "A jerk that I'm about to kill."

"Really?" Evan stands in front of the door just as I move to walk out of it. "You're going to walk down there with God knows what, flinging around this place and go with all guns blazing?" He pauses to read my reaction. "And then what? Yell because he decided to get with another girl, seriously?" It's rhetorical, and I'm thinking about punching him in the face too whilst I'm at it.

He knows this and continues speaking. "It's more logical to think of some pretty good revenge. Play the innocent girlfriend and kick him the fucking balls when he's cowering and, on all fours—"

"You're disgusting."

"If you let me finish you would know I was going to say metaphorically."

"I don't want to hear it."

"Because the truth hurts, baby."

"The truth doesn't hurt." I groan. "It's the wave of emotion that claws at you after it that kills."

"Jesus Christ." He starts to laugh. "Where did you get that from?"

"Don't be a dick." But I can't help but feel kind of embarrassed I said it.

Evan smirks, the corners of his lips curving. "Then stop making me be one."

I try to change the subject. "Oh, for God's sake, it's hardly my fault you're useless."

"I'm useless?" Evan pulls a face. "I'm sorry, but who is the one that enlightened you on your cheating and indescribably idiot of a boyfriend?"

"On that note…" I begin moving towards the door. Evan doesn't stop me; he can't because the door is already flying open and six-armed guards file through, shining their flashlights on our faces.

I hide my eyes from the lights and glance over at Evan. "What the *hell* is going on?"

•　　　•　　　•

We were sent back to our room, escorted and watched as we rolled into our sleeping bags and blankets and settled down. I try to make as little noise as possible, realizing that the weather outside is growing more thunderous as time passes. A glass shard sticks up at the tip of my finger, but I'm pretending to be asleep, so I can't lodge it out. My eyes are closed, and I try to even out my breathing. A security guard kicks the side of my rib as he walks past, and I hold in my urge to yelp.

Murmurs of voices start to trickle through the momentary silence. I can hear them speaking, something in Italian. Some of us took Italian classes freshmen to junior year, but I haven't ever had to focus on something so hard to figure out what they are saying. I pick up some words and try to string a sentence together.

"The women won't survive this storm," one had said, "All they do is cry."

I roll over and allow my left leg to roll with me, and I kick one of them as I do.

"Ohi!"

"Va bene, lei è ancora addormentata."

I don't know what they're saying, but they eventually leave, assured we are both asleep. My eyes open as the door shuts and I sit up, squinting through the black room. I spot Ben's empty sleeping bag right in the corner, barely noticeable with every other student crammed in. But I can see it's empty, and it stays empty for the rest of the night.

•　　•　　•

"Wake up, Kayla."

"Kayla, wake the hell up!"

I groan. "Huh?"

"Ben's missing."

I blink enough to allow myself to see, and rub my eyes. I must have fallen asleep because the light is seeping through the crack in the door and the storm only blows in the heavy wind. I sit up slowly, scanning the room as if Ben will suddenly reappear.

"What?" I finally say when I can see Sophie's waiting for my reply. She's leaning over me and steps back as I sit up, her expression pale. Her mom's Mexican, so her naturally tanned skinned makes me jealous. I wish I had some sort of Hispanic descent.

"Sophie," I prompt her this time, "what's happening?"

"Apparently Ben has been missing since last night, so is Jessica Beech." She eyes me warily as I take in this information. So last night wasn't a dream then.

Even so, I try to act surprised. "Jess Beech?"

"Yeah." She tries to read my reaction again, but she looks edgy, and I know she's thinking the same thing I already know.

"You don't think the storm…" I hold my breath, my thoughts making a mess inside my brain, tripping over each other to think of a logical conclusion. I can feel sweat pooling on the back of my neck and I know I'm worried. Hell, I can't stop myself. I've spent three years in love with Ben Moore to not be worried—his cheating ass or not. But the worry clouds with anger and I don't know which one I feel more. He should be back by now.

"Don't think like that." Sophie shakes her head defiantly and sits cross-legged beside me. "They're both absolutely fine. They *have* to be."

"But they're *together*, Soph," I whisper. "They're definitely sleeping together."

"What?" She gawks at me in utter shock, her face displaying a card of confusion, anger, and apprehensiveness. I know she doesn't know where to look when she finally drops her gaze, so I sigh and try to explain to her how I know.

"I heard someone leaving the room last night, and I could have sworn it was Ben. So, I got up, followed him. I found Evan Winters instead eating a bag of chips, and he pointed to the end of the corridor…" I trail off and look around me to make sure I wasn't in earshot of any prying students. This was embarrassing enough. "There he was, Soph, just right there kissing *her*. I'm a…what do you say? *Moron*. I am a moron, a complete and utter idiot."

Sophie is pulling me into a hug as I try to blink back the tears that threaten to spill. I squeeze them shut and try to think of anything else but Ben Moore. But all I can see when my eyes close is his lips on hers.

Sophie starts to push back, and she gives me a look. "But wait," she frowns, "did you say Evan Winters showed you?"

"Yeah."

"Evan?"

"Yes, Sophie."

"But you two hate each other. Like *hate*. It's kinda crazy."

I snort. "Hate's a strong word…extremely dislike the opposite person? Yes."

Sophie smiles. "Funny how the person you dislike most in the world was actually the person who was more of a friend to you at the moment you needed, eh?" She tries to look distracted and ties the laces of her shoes, but they are already tied.

"I wouldn't say a friend," I make a face, "he wasn't exactly nice about it."

"Well, he showed you, Kayla. If he really hated you, he'd let you go on whilst he knew this information and make you look like a proper idiot." Sophie says, making a point. "Anyway, that's Evan's girlfriend there too."

"They aren't together," I tell her pointedly.

"What?"

"Yeah, my reaction exactly. Apparently, it was a rumor he never thought was important enough to squash." I shrug.

Sophie shakes her head and then leans out to touch my knee. "I wish there was something I could say to make you feel better." She squeezes my knee as she says it and I try to force a smile.

So do I, Soph, so do I.

• • •

It's half past ten that morning when we are called on as a group. Mrs. Scott looks a state this morning, crazy hair and coriander from last night's soup stuck in her teeth. I can't really blame her; we are all a hot mess, and she's doing her best to keep us calm. We gather around her and the other teachers.

"As you might have seen, there are eight security men here alongside our group. The fact of the matter is: we are stuck in the waiting rooms in the airport. Therefore, duty-free shop and the food courts are not available to us. The storm looks better than last night; however, I have heard that it is still unsafe to venture out just yet."

A collective groan fills the room.

"I'm hopeful that tonight will be our last night here, but in order to do that, we must keep our spirits high and remain together." We all look around the room at each other, and I can tell nobody's spirits have been high since we arrived. This trip was supposed to be the first in our schools 'educational foreign experiences' and is offered to seniors with good GPA averages and behavior records. Instead, it looks like half the school board was right—this doesn't work.

Mrs. Scott continues, "Therefore, as we deploy some of you to search for the next round of food, you all make sure that you've changed into clean clothes and made yourselves feel a little more presentable. I know it's the last thing you want to do in this situation but feeling clean makes you feel good, and boy don't we need a lot of that." She claps her hands, and just like that the group begins to disperse from the huddle we formed.

I drift back to where Sophie and I have placed our stuff and think of what she said. It bothers me that she hadn't mentioned Ben's or Jess's disappearance. If Sophie noticed, she definitely would have done. I'm so consumed with the thought of it. I don't even realize someone has been calling my name until they tug me on the shoulder.

"Whoa." I trip slightly, snapping out of my tangent of thoughts.

"I need your help." Evan's blinking at me.

"Why?"

"Didn't you hear what she said?" Evan asks. He speaks to me like I'm stupid. "The food court isn't available to us."

"Yeah…I know?"

"Well, we need to make it available."

"What are you saying?"

Evan seems frustrated with my misunderstanding. "I'm saying you need to grab that tall legged British friend of yours and I'll take my guys and we're finding a decent meal for us and the group."

"You want to try and break into the food court?" I confirm.

"Exactly. You got it in one."

"Then why do you need me?" I frown.

"Because we are making a pit stop." He smiles. "We'll look for Ben and Jess on the way."

Chapter Four

Surprisingly, Sophie jumps at the idea to break into the food court, despite pointing out multiple times that it would mean breaking the law, not to mention highly dangerous. She didn't seem to consider the fact we'd have to find a way to *get* there, and that meant finding a way from this building to the main one, which meant going through the storm. I also made a valid point throughout this conversation that Evan Winters would also be leading this with his master plan (he has yet to share) and thus making the entire thing even crazier than it already sounds. But Sophie Carson is nothing but trusting and convincing. So of course, I go.

Damon and Tom Clare are twins and Evan's best friends. It's like jocks meet the wombats because each of them doesn't stereotypically mesh together. But it kind of just *works*. For some reason, that's the allure about them. They have been inseparable since eighth grade when Damon had announced he was gay. It had been one of the most surreal moments of eighth grade. Damon had climbed onto the lunch hall table and bellowed his confession from his chest like something out of *The Lion King*. Of course, he'd got a lot of sniggers, mean comments and I remember someone throwing something at him. Even back then, Evan had watched from the sidelines as usual, and instead of belittling him like the others,

Evan had been the one to support him. For a split second, I allowed myself to like him. I admired him.

That feeling hasn't happened since.

Sophie's motherly sigh interupts me from my thinking. "Seriously, Kayla, live a little. We haven't just flown thousands of miles to be stuck in these four walls. We're all hungry, and we are doing this for everyone. We can't be selfish." She sounds stern. Her lips turn up into a grin and she knows she's caught me out on this one.

"You have a point."

"Of course, I do." She smiles smugly. "So, suck it up, baby girl, and let's go find the boys."

•   •   •

It's around eight when the plan is supposed to begin. And I say *supposed to* because Mrs. Scott ends up recruiting Evan's group in the water run. It revolves around a bucket and a shit load of rainwater which I am not sure is even hygienic.

"Too bad" —I said, leaning against the wall with my eyes closed— "guess that means no breaking in." I'm trying not to sound smug, or like a bitch, but I can't deny that it makes me feel relieved. I peek at Sophie out of the corner of my eye and she's glaring at me with such intensity I feel the urge to shut them again.

"Enough with the sarcasm, Kayla." She fiddles with the ends of her hair and looks over her shoulder at a student who brushes past. "I'm sick of you moping around and being such a Debby Downer. This situation is less than ideal, and I know that you're going through some crap with Ben, but it's important for all of us to eat. We're all pissed and hungry and Evan might be a right prick but he's actually making an effort, and you've got to give the kid some credit for that."

"Wow." I breathe out shortly, surprised by her outburst. I shift on the floor, feeling uncomfortable and considering she may even have a point. He was trying, and I guess that's all anyone can ask for.

"Not wow, Kayla," she says. "Just help us."

"Okay, I'm down." I hold my hands up in surrender and try to not show my reluctance. I know she's right which only makes me feel worse. I haven't considered the bigger picture and what doing this could mean for anyone else. I've been thinking selfishly and if this was anyone else's idea other than Evan Winters I might have been more for it. I try to show willing, and stand up, eyeing Mrs. Scott from across the room. I can feel Sophie hot on my trail as I approach my teacher and tap her shoulder.

"Do you mind if Sophie and I help?" I ask her with a smile.

"What?" Mrs. Scott turns, her short hair bobbing against her shoulders. She looks between Sophie and I and then towards the other end of the room where Evan and his friends have come back. "You want to help Evan and the others?" She looks at me curiously, like she's waiting for the punch line of a bad joke. I guess teachers have also recognized our shared hatred for each other.

I start to nod and force a smile to sell it to her. "I do."

"You sure?" Mrs. Scott eyes me and then looks at Sophie as if she needs confirmation. I see Sophie give her a flattering grin and our teacher begins to purse her lips.

"Yes, Mrs. Scott. I'm sure,"

"Okay then, but you better go now because the boys have a lot to do." Mrs. Scott ushers us away and Sophie squeezes my shoulder.

"Damn girl, you are a good actor." She gives me a little wink, and I laugh.

"Common let's go save some stomachs."

$$\bullet \qquad \bullet \qquad \bullet$$

"That stuff stinks," I say between the choked coughs. Evan's cigarette dangles from his mouth, the ash falling to the floor as the cigarette burns further. He leans in, pulling at my waist and then takes a long drag of the cigarette before blowing the smoke into my face. I'm too repulsed I can barely stumble backward and try to bat the smoke away from my face with my hand.

"You're beyond disgusting." I grimace, the taste of tobacco on my lips.

"Thank you, darling," he mimics a Southern accent and licks his lips, dropping the cigarette from his teeth and rubbing his shoe over it.

"*Ugh.*"

"Will you two stop flirting with each other and come on over here and help us!" Damon yells. He's tall, at least six foot two with dyed brown hair. He rocks a pair of green eyes that make just about every girl wish he wasn't gay and a sense of fashion you only see models wear on catwalks.

Tom, on the other hand, is brilliantly intelligent, and with the type of look that goes with it. He wears black-rimmed glasses that frame his face and a pair of Converse that are quite literally stuck to his feet. I don't think I've ever seen the boy in another other than his pair. Not in the gym, not at school dances, not ever. He and his brother share their height as well as their extremely annoying knack for making people like them. They keep to themselves mostly, but I've worked with them both on school projects, and they are too likable for their own good.

"We are not flirting with each other," I say defensively as Evan and I join the others.

Evan looks at me sideways, as if to say *are you kidding?* And makes a face at Damon. "Really? Her?" But he's grinning a grin that creeps me out.

"Right," Tom says, his arms wrapped around a bucket of water. "So, here's the plan…"

•　　　•　　　•

Armed with a tree stump and a makeshift pick made from bobby pins, I slowly make my way around the glass that scatters aimlessly on the floor and slip into the space where Evan and Sophie stand. The security guards are crawling all over this place, and it's clear that trying to find an escape out of the steel door towards the terminals is going to be anything but easy.

The wind has died down but has been replaced by torrential rain. Each drop announces itself on the building, thunderous and loud. Each piece of broken glass that crunches beneath our feet makes each of us inhale sharply as if we are waiting for the ground to give way beneath us. I feel on edge more than ever, my heart faltering in my chest and my ears ringing. I want to turn back and join the others, but it's too late now.

"I'll go first," Evan whispers, turning so we can hear him. He shoots me a glance and then says, "then Kayla." I only nod my response.

Evan turns to the others, so they can hear him better. "You three wait five minutes and then do the same, but please make sure you aren't seen. I have no idea how we would explain this without it looking fishy."

The others nod, and Evan steps out of our hiding place and disappears down the black corridor. I wait for a minute, nod at Sophie, Damon, and Tom, and slip out the door and down the same corridor.

I don't like the dark. I never have. It's unnerving, not being able to see properly and have every other sense heightened. I can hear each breath; every step I take like I am hearing sound for the first time. I can taste the cold soup from last night in my mouth and feel the beads of sweat form on my palms. I don't really know where I'm going which makes this whole thing worse. I can barely see, which makes every step a guess in which way I am going. I look over my shoulder as if someone's standing there, lurking in the darkness but of course I can't see anything.

So, I start to walk faster, do a slow jog. From Evan's scouting earlier, he had told us that there would be an adjoining corridor that is a back passage for staff to reach the terminals and duty-free. I don't know how he knows all of this, he doesn't seem like the type to care enough about this sort of thing, but the boy is right, and I have to give him that. I reach my left hand out and try to hold onto the wall as I walk, the visibility slowly diminishing with each second.

I start to smell smoke, and I'm convinced that I've gone the wrong way. I'm panicking, my hand shaking against the wall.

"Shit."

"There's no need to swear," Evan's voice rings in my ears, and I reach out to find him. His back is turned to me, and I grab his neck out of sheer desperation and pull him around, relieved that I've found him. It's a feeling I never thought I'd experience. Evan Winters giving *me* relief.

"Oh, God, don't tell me you're scared of the dark," he murmurs. It's dark so I can't really see his face, but I can tell he's smiling by the way he speaks. "You're such a girl."

"Opposed to anything else?" I say irritably. "As you're a sexist pig, but we aren't all pointing out the obvious."

Evan chuckles. "Nothing I' haven't heard before."

I fist balls up, and I have to tell myself to calm down, so it relaxes. "Then why not take it on board, change yourself?" I'm whispering to him but it's loud, or maybe it's because the corridor is so dark. Our voices bounce off the walls. I can vaguely see Evan fiddling with something in his hand, something silver, metallic.

"Kayla, please." His tone suggests he's bored. "I need to concentrate. I don't need an equality lecture right now." He steps aside and pushes against the door. The handle is broken when I reach out and feel.

I roll my eyes despite knowing he won't see. "I wasn't—"

"Kayla, your shirt literally says *Equal pay is fair game.*" He starts to chuckle. "You're the epitome of lectures, stop forcing your opinion on everyone else."

"And?" I'm trying not to be offended.

"*And* I don't need this right now. You're like one of those Christians that forces Jesus on you. I'm not a feminist and I believe equality can only go so far. It's my opinion, alright? Isn't it in the handbook that we are all entitled to that?" He pushes against the door now. I don't answer him. I don't know what to say. "Besides, we need to find Ben and Jess," he adds like he's trying to change the subject.

"You miss her," I confirm from my deductions of the past few days.

"What?" Evan sounds surprised.

"Jess, you miss her," I repeat.

I hear him scoff. "What are you talking about?"

"Oh, come on, it's obvious. You always seem so tense when she is the topic of the conversation. I noticed it on the plane and earlier with the others and even just now. *You miss her.* And despite the fact you're not going out with her, you still like her," I pause, but he doesn't say anything, so I continue. "It bothers you that she has gone somewhere with Ben. In fact, I'd put money on it that it bothers you just as much as it bothers me."

He remains silent, not even moving so I reach out to touch his arm and he freezes just as I do. I don't really know where I'm going with this anymore, but the words pool out of my lips before I can stop them.

"That's why you showed me. And it wasn't because you were being a jerk, but because I'm the only one that can relate to your pain. It was your idea to find her. And as much as you pretend not to care about anything, it hurts you that she's just upped and left, probably making out in some room with my boyfriend. You want to be there with her, that's why you never declined or suppressed those rumors about her being your girlfriend. You *want* her to be yours." I let out a breath and Evan starts to push against the door, ignoring me for what feels like forever.

I don't say anything else but watch his dark figure push against the door until he stops and faces me. The corridor is tight, and his chest bumps against mine, and we both pull away at the same time.

Evan's voice is low as he speaks, "Don't presume to know my feelings, Kayla. It isn't what you think." But I can feel his hand reach out, and I don't know if it's by accident, but he brushes his fingers over mine. His hand drops quicker than it happens, and I know we will never be the best of friends, but I think it's something.

Chapter Five

It turns out that the door doesn't budge like steel: hard as hell and completely frustrating. There are five of us pushing at it and it doesn't move an inch. It's like pushing at air: nothing happens.

Damon also seems full of ridiculous ideas tonight. He first suggested we tried lifting the door from the bottom as if we're the Incredible Hulk. He then suggested we use the bobby pin picks we made earlier to pick the lock, which seemed like a great idea until we all realized that all we were doing was double locking it further.

Damon steps forward into the small shred of light, his shoe crunching over some glass. "Maybe if we try..."

"No." We all chorus.

I release a heavy sigh and slump against the door, careful to avoid any glass. The metal is cold on my back and tickles the tips of the hairs on my neck. I'm all about giving up and I knew this idea was absurd from the start. I can't even pretend to go along with it now.

"It's no use," Tom moans. It's the first time he's spoken for a while and I see his shadowy figure looming behind Evan. "The door is made from reinforced steel or some shit."

Sophie knocks into me, clearly by accident, but her hand finds my shoulder and clamps down, squeezing. I don't have to see her to know her mind is spinning; she's trying to think of another idea. We all are.

"What about if we—"

"Damon, dude," Evan shoots his friend down, "we've literally tried everything. I can't see anything that could help, I can't fucking see *anything* at all. It's not gonna work."

"I was gonna say," Damon's voice has a hint of laughter slipping through it, "if we press this emergency button, wouldn't the door just open?"

I'm on my feet before he finishes his sentence. "You're joking, right?" I try to stop the giggle. "Just hit it."

Damon does. I move away from the door quickly as the sound of heavy metal rattles upward, and a string of light floods through the corridor.

"Holy shit." Tom shields his eyes. "I can't believe there was a button there this entire time."

The door begins to slowly open from the bottom, beads of light suddenly filling the corridor. I begin to blink to make my eyes readjust. I've been staring into darkness for so long. It's like waking up in a dark room and looking at your phone; you're so blind for a moment that it takes a while to adjust.

But I wish I hadn't.

The door opens further, and my eyes suddenly adjust to the light. The cold air hits me, but it isn't the only thing that does. Outside is a mess. An utter mess. Trees decorate the runways, overturned trucks and cars line the corners, and a head of a plane has crashed through one exterior building. Pools of water so deep I could swim around on the uneven ground and from where we stand, I can see…

"I think I'm going to be sick," Sophie whispers next to me. I know she can see it too.

"They're not..." but Tom trails off, "that isn't..."

"A dead body," Damon murmurs from behind, and I gulp down the growing feeling of sickness.

"There's probably more," Evan echoes, his voice sounds restraint, choked.

"We need to move." Tom walks past us and slaps his brother on the shoulder. Damon stumbles forward slightly. *"Now."*

He's right. A small hurricane has formed in the distance, and I know it's only a matter of time before it will reach us. I can feel myself start to panic, the apprehension claws at me and I try to calm myself down by thinking of the goal.

"Come on," Damon yells and bursts out into the storm. It's raining like I've never seen rain before and being in it is even more surreal. This entire thing has me gasping for air as Damon starts to lead us outside. I can't even comprehend the fact I am voluntarily out here. I feel as if I'm watching myself from a distance like I'm not even here. But this is real; it's all too real.

"Pick it up a bit," Evan roars at us over the sound of the wind and the rain. I can barely see; my hair is soaked against my face, and the wind pulls me in all and every direction. I clutch at my jacket and pull it further around me for warmth, but it does little to help.

Evan now leads. He's running fast and heading towards a broken door in the building opposite. I can just make it out. The end is near. I start to let myself feel slightly relieved just as a gust of wind knocks me to my feet. I crash to the ground and struggle to pull myself up, each breath feeling like it's been knocked out of me. I have no strength, and I consider for a second that they should all just leave me out here, but I can feel their hands pull at me and I'm suddenly standing. Evan has looped his arm through mine and is pulling me with him but I'm so gasped for air I feel like I'm barely moving.

But then we hit the other side and we push through, knocking the door completely off its hinges, but the running doesn't stop there. We are still vulnerable to the storm here and there's no time to take a breather. Evan's clutching me so hard, and I'm so convinced he believes he can't let go because his grip tightens as my breathing quickens. I can hear the others beside us, and we run for what feels like forever, bursting through a maze of corridors and hallways.

It's a century before I feel like we are safe enough, and I let go of Evan as we all haul ourselves over the security gates and towards the duty-free logos. I consider for the first time since we came in here that we haven't seen another person. Not a security guard or staff worker, not even a passenger. Not a single soul.

"It's there!" Tom yells and snaps me back into focus. We slowly jog to the entrance, and I realize we haven't seen anyone because they are all here.

Hundreds of people swarm inside, and that's only from what I can see. Most of the duty-free has been looted, and the rest lay scattered on the floor destroyed. I can't see food anywhere, but I can smell it and my stomach protests at me in hunger.

The others feel it too.

"Shit, we didn't think this through." Evan punches the door. "They aren't just going to hand us the food, are they?"

"Jesus Christ," Sophie moans for the first time since this plan was put in action. "I thought you had thought of everything, Evan."

"Clearly not," I say slyly under my breath.

"They have to help us," Tom says with a point. "They aren't monsters."

"What do we do?" Damon questions. He sounds as wheezed as I feel.

"We go in." Before I can think any more of it, I push the door open and start to walk in. I can hear the others call my name, but I don't turn around. I walk . . . faster.

"Does anyone here speak English?" I announce. I can hear the door open from behind, and I know the others must be behind. The further I walk, the bigger I see how the duty-free area is. A couple of heads turn to face me. A guy steps out from the crowd, dressed in a shirt and suit pants. He wears a lanyard around his neck. He looks as if he works here.

"I do," the guy says to me. I can tell he's British, and I'm momentarily relieved. "I'm also fluent in Italian. Everyone else here is Polish or French. I haven't been able to really get through. Any chance you speak either?"

I stare at him for a moment and take in what he says. "Uh sure, I know French."

"That's great, you might have to stand on something to get everyone to listen," the British guy pulls out a chair, and I climb onto it.

"What are you doing?" Tom is beside me, looking up.

"I am speaking French?" It comes out more like a question than a statement and I clear my throat before I begin in a loud voice.

"Um, hello, my name's Kayla, and I and my senior class are trapped over in the other building opposite," I explain, pointing to the window. My French is rusty, so I struggle and not sure if all my tenses are correct, but I continue. "We haven't eaten anything, and I know there are a lot of you, but if you could spare anything we'd be so grateful."

I suck in a breath and look around. Some of the people look puzzled, but a vast majority seem to have some understanding of what I'm saying. "I know this is a difficult time, we are all scared and in a country that we aren't familiar with, but we need to help each other."

"At the moment, our friends are stuck in that building, but we found a way out. Hopefully, we can go back and get them to join you here, but we need to take something back if that's all okay with everyone."

The Best Part Of Hello | 36

A sudden deafening silence engulfs the room but at the same time, I feel as if I can hear everyone's minds buzzing at the same time. The British guy eyes the crowd and I watch him read their reactions. "Of course, we will help. It's not every man for himself."

My shoulders sag and the tension I didn't realize I had been holding in diminishes. "Thank you." I step down from the chair and move it to where it was earlier. I turn to my friends and they all look at me, dumbfounded.

"Since when did you speak French?" Sophie looks at me like we are meeting for the first time.

I shrug. "My grandparents are French, so we learned it from a young age."

"Right, as you do." She shakes her head and laughs, but she's interrupted by a horror-filled shriek that comes from the back of the room. The crowd begins to part, and I see a woman cowering over a small boy on the floor just as foam starts to pour out of his mouth.

"Oh, my God," Evan's voice is the only thing I can hear before the woman starts to yell again.

"Help!" she screams. "Help him!" So she speaks English too.

Something unknown to me compels me to run over. I barge through the crowd of people until I reach the little boy and my stomach knots as more foam starts to pour from his mouth. I have only limited medical knowledge, mostly from bad TV shows and the books I've read. Nursing was something I had always been interested in but watching something on TV compared to the real deal is completely different. It takes a second for me to realize that someone else had joined me, and it's the British guy from earlier. He's rolled up his sleeves, and an army-style tattoo covers his right lower arm. He doesn't look at all flustered by this situation which makes me think he knows what he's doing.

"Are you a doctor?" I ask, leaning down at the boy's feet.

"Trainee surgeon for the marines, but it's about the same," he says as he concentrates on the boy's pulse.

"Airways?" I query as I notice the British guy open his mouth further and then place his ear to his chest.

The British guy doesn't look up at me but speaks, "They're blocked. Something is lodged." He opens his briefcase I hadn't even noticed until now and pulls out a weird looking instrument.

I look towards the boy's mother and stare at her intensely. "What has he eaten?"

"What?" She wipes away her tears as another woman tries to console her.

"What has he eaten?" I repeat, a little less patient than before.

"One of these." She digs into her purse and tosses me a wrapper. It's in Italian, so I've not got a clue what it says.

"Okay." I flap the wrapper in the British guy's face, and he looks up at me finally. "Read the ingredients," I demand.

"Oh, um…" Nervously he does and bites his lip, eyeing the boy as he starts to convulse. The pressure is on, and I hope it's what I think it is. "Eggs, dark chocolate, hazelnut—"

"Hazelnut!" The mother cries. "He's allergic."

"Do you have an EpiPen on you?" The British guy quizzes, tilting the boys head back ever so slightly. The foaming has stopped and has instead been replaced with scarier convulsions.

"Uh…" she trails off and looks around as if one would magically appear. "No, I haven't. God, I knew I forgot something."

Something inside of me snaps. "What parent doesn't carry around an EpiPen for their child with severe allergies?" I clench my fists.

"Hey, hey." The British guy grabs my hands and steadies me. I didn't realize until now that I'm shaking. "It isn't her fault. It happens."

I take a deep breath and nod, looking over at the boy's mom who's beside herself and I apologize. "I'm sorry, that wasn't fair." But I don't think she's really listening.

British guy nods and chews his bottom lip in thought. "If we don't have an EpiPen, we're going to have to try something else."

"Like what?" I question.

"Like making sure that he can breathe."

I push my hair out of my face and try to stop myself from panicking any more than I am already. "How are we going to do that?"

"He needs a shot of adrenaline. His anaphylactic shock is getting worse," British guy explains. "Hold this." He produces a needle from his briefcase and presses it into my hand.

"On my count, stick it into him here," he instructs, pointing to his thigh. I stare at him, completely thrown.

"Wait, what, you want me to inject him?" It's a question that I already know the answer to.

"Yes," he confirms. "I need to unblock his airways."

Trembling, I nod and wait for him to hold the boy's mouth firmly open. "On the count of three: one, two, three."

I jab the needle inside the boy's thigh and press down to release the liquid. Adrenaline kicks through my veins like the one I am administering to him, and I'm left staring at the boy, waiting for something to happen. Thirty seconds feels like thirty years and when the boy finally stops convulsing, his body stilling. Another thirty seconds pass, and dread feels my bones as he doesn't move. I can feel the apprehension in the air as we all watch. His mom cries harder, her sobs choked.

"He's—" but just as she starts, the boy begins coughing violently, but pushes himself up into a sitting position and I push away, the relief swarming through every particle of my body.

"Mother of God," Damon's voice echoes behind me. "This girl is crazy."

Chapter Six

Adam. The cute British guy is called Adam. His East London accent, information courtesy of Sophie, is dreamy. I just want him to carry on talking, much like how I used to be with Sophie.

"So, you're a trainee surgeon in the army?" I reconfirm, crossing my legs on the floor. We haven't moved since helping the little boy.

"Yeah," he says. Adam sits with his back pressed against the wall as he sorts through his briefcase. The others have gone to get us some food. "Though I was meant to come out to Rome to extend my training."

"Is there any way you can get in contact with anyone? I mean, I know over at the building we were in, the lines were down, and all the phones were broken by the storm…"

"It's the same here, Kayla," he interrupts.

"Right." I feel defeated.

"It's weird, you know," he says with a frown, "not being able to contact anyone. I feel like we've gone back years." I watch as a wrinkle folds in his forehead, a thought troubling him.

I can tell he's older, in his early twenties or so and my eyes drift down to his hand I am thrilled to see he's not married. I try to tell myself to stop it; he's older, he's also ridiculously cute, which doesn't help matters further. He's cuteness comes from his mess of brown hair and dark grey eyes. Freckles decorate his nose, the underneath of his eyes and when he smiles, he shows his teeth.

"I know," I agree after a moment of gathering my thoughts.

He coughs, trying to change the subject and peeks at me through his thick eyelashes. "Anyway…"

"Um, yeah…" I stand up awkwardly and hover. "I should be getting to my friends." I force a smile and turn away, my cheeks flushing as I turn too quick and knock into a chair. This boy is literally knocking me off my feet and I barely met him five minutes ago.

It takes me longer than I'd like to admit to reach the others. They all stand in a small huddle conversing in small voices. Damon's got his lips around something long, it dangles from his mouth and from a distance it looks like jerky, up close it smells more like candy. I'm so focused on it that I don't realize they have all seen me coming until Evan speaks.

"Oh, here comes the hero," he scowls at me sarcastically and his lips turn into a smirk when I glare back. Sophie spins around and engulfs me into a hug. A chunk of her hair gets stuck in my mouth and I have to scramble to pull it away, my hands trapped at my sides.

"That was incredible," she says, her voice void of sarcasm. "I have never seen anything like it! It was like watching an episode of *Grey's Anatomy*."

"It was scary," I admit, and she pulls away and frowns.

"Why?"

"Because if I didn't do something right, that little boy could have died in my arms," I explain. I shake the thought away. I don't know what I was doing there in the first place. "Anyway, Adam told me that a large majority of the staff got out."

"What? How?" Damon stops chewing.

I shrug. "I don't know, but he said he hasn't been able to find a single person who works here for days."

"But you said the large majority?" Evan butts in with a frown.

I make a face, "well the ones he found were..." but I trail off because it doesn't take a genius to know what I am saying. He found them dead.

"It's insane, bloody stupid!" Sophie cries. We get a few dirty looks from a family with children in the corner, and I try to smile an apology. "How can they just leave us?"

"Maybe it wasn't a choice," Tom pipes up. "Maybe it was just their procedure."

"Well, shouldn't they have a procedure for all of us?" Evan says what we are all thinking.

"Look I'm sure they do," Tom reassures. "I mean they know we are here, right? They aren't just going to leave us all here. The government won't allow it, and aren't airports like one of the first places they try to evacuate?"

"He's got a point," Sophie says with a grin. "Full of wise words, aren't ya?"

We all grin and Tom walks away. I look over my shoulder to see Adam in a conversation with a woman. "He wants us to stay."

"Who does?" Evan says but follows my gaze. "Why you all gooey eyed? Hey! You barely know the guy."

"Why do you care?" I fire back as Damon says, "We can't right now."

Evan rolls his eyes at me, "I don't, and Damon's right, we can't stay with your new boyfriend because we are here to bring food back to our class, not drum up a romance. Besides, we gotta find Jess and Ben; they are still on a walkabout."

"We have to find some sort of way to signal at them." Sophie compromises and stares out of one of the windows towards the building we had been in. "We can't go back out there, not tonight, it seems to be getting worse."

"She's right." Tom appears with five steaming cups of coffee and hands one to me. I am so hungry that I am contemplating eating the takeout cup.

I smile at him gratefully and face the others. "We need to do something."

"There's no point in overthinking it now," Damon butts in, "it's almost midnight." The sky is dark, the only light illuminated from a window in the opposite building and a couple of unbroken lights that line the runway. I fiddle with my sleeve jacket and think back to the others and how hungry they must be. Each sip of my coffee makes me feel guilty. I know Mrs. Scott must be freaking out by now; this is seven students she has now lost, and she is after all, still responsible for us despite the majority of my classmates are eighteen and therefore, adults.

I push the thoughts away and the guilt that comes with them too and Damon points to a group of empty chairs which seems to be our bed for the night. They line the unbroken window and look as comfy as a box of rocks.

"So," he says finally. "Who wants a chair?"

But it isn't a chair I wake up on.

Hours later…

It's freezing. Fucking freezing. It's as if my body is submerged in ice, tearing at my skin and drowning me. I try to move, but my body doesn't do as it's asked, and I feel paralyzed, each muscle, each bone stuck. And then there is the pain, and I think it's coming from my leg. I am in agony and I'm screaming, except I don't think I'm making any noise.

"Quickly!" I'm aware of someone yelling in the distance, but I can't make out what they are saying properly as the voice comes closer. "It's getting worse!"

"Kayla!" someone shouts, a new voice. And then, "oh crap, *help!*"

The next thing I know, I'm being lifted. But the sensation of being on fire suddenly rips through my body, as if I'm being burned alive. The coldness seeps away and the burning sensation leaves me withering in more pain. I wish for the cold, for the bliss against this.

"Oh shit," someone says. "This is really, really bad."

Walking. I'm walking—but of course, I'm not. I can't move my legs. I can't even open my eyes. Someone else must be carrying me, someone else walking. I try to force myself to stay conscious, to be aware of my surroundings, of what's going on. I need to stay awake. I know this, but everything suddenly feels so heavy.

Maybe a lot of time passes, I couldn't tell you. The next thing I am aware of is feeling numb and so very cold again, the burning has stopped. I try to tell myself to be relieved that it's over, but the cold engulfs my body so much so I must be a statue. I even try to open my eyes, but all I see is stars.

"She keeps drifting in and out of consciousness," a voice says quietly. "It's bad, look at how deep."

"She's bleeding out," another voice confirms, one I start to recognize. But it doesn't matter what's said after that, I have no hope of hearing. The stars that cloud my vision disappear, and then it all goes black.

·   ·   ·

Something's buzzing, and then a voice comes into focus and the buzzing is muted.

"Wake up, Kayla. Goddammit. You've always been so stubborn but even for you, this is effort isn't it? Jesus Christ girl, you cannot die on me. You can't die like *this*. It's not fair. How the hell would I explain this?" I make out a low chuckle and then the smell of cigarette smoke. The voice starts again after a pause. "Who am I going to vent my frustration to other than you?"

It's Evan Winters, and I want to punch him, so I must be back to my old self. I tell myself not to move, but I can feel everything again as if my body is back. I do everything to stop myself from making a noise and just listen.

"It's been three days now, Kayla, you've got to wake up. Think about your mom, your dad, and your brother back at home." The smell of cigarettes fills my nostrils again and I do everything in my power to avoid gagging as he continues. "Shit, what the hell am I supposed to say?" he is asking someone else. Someone else is in the room.

"Think of a memory." It's another male's voice, a British one: Adam.

"Oh god, um…" Evan finds my hand, and I freeze. Jesus Evan, this wasn't a part of the deal. Trying to act dead whilst the boy you don't like touches you is kind of impossible. "Last winter your mom made my mom this casserole thing with that really nice beef topping that was crunchy and…*God*, what am I saying? Uh…but anyway, I had walked upstairs and saw you next door in just your robe and dancing to some nauseatingly old Madonna number, and I mean… *Christ* girl, your music taste is awful." He laughs to himself as the memory becomes more prominent and I try to think back to what he's talking about and bite the insides of my cheeks to stop the flush of embarrassment that threatens them.

"But there you were, standing in your robe, doing this fist pump dance move that was getting you really into the song. I remember thinking that I had the urge to climb over that tree that separates our two houses and come and join you."

He coughs, and the room feels awkward. "I'm not saying that I like you, in fact, you're completely unbearable and neurotic, and I can't stand you most of the time. But even I realized then that you're not *that* bad, and if you could evoke that sort of weird emotion in me, then maybe you're a tiny bit less neurotic after all." He lets go of my hand and stands up. I can hear the chair he was sitting on screeching against the floor and the door opening and closing.

"Wow," a voice whispers. Then I realize it's me.

Chapter Seven

It's Friday the thirteenth, and I'm fourteen again. It was one of the worst but also one of the best years of my life. It was the year Evan moved in next door. The old couple who used to live there needed to downsize, but God I missed them. Years of babysitting and being read stories to in funny voices were something the fourteen-year-old me was going to miss; even if I didn't want to admit it. Our seemingly quiet neighborhood was now replaced by the sound of another fourteen-year-old boy arguing with his little sister. *All the time.* But that year wasn't all bad. The best thing that happened was Ben Moore asking me out. Ben Moore, complete heartthrob even at that age, and he chose *me.* I pretty much fainted. I had never been so happy. He did it in front of everyone, put on a big show of announcing it in class. I was half humiliated and half ecstatic…okay maybe more ecstatic.

But for some reason, it's the year I can't stop thinking about now. It's the year that everything changed.

I'm certainly *not* thrilled that I am awake again, because the pain is back, just duller. Sophie is sitting on the metal slab that I have now figured out is a kitchen worktop which means we must be in some kind of staff kitchen. She's got her head in her hands and is mumbling something repeatedly under her breath. The air smells stale, metallic, and worn as if someone has sucked all the energy out of it. I try to raise my head and bend my knee, but a shooting pain from my leg fires at the nerves in my body, and in shock. I fling my head back quickly onto the table. The racket I make stops Sophie from doing whatever it was, and she gawps at me, long and hard, as if she is waiting for me to fall back asleep—or die. I can't tell. It's like she's imagining it.

Her gawping turns into a large smile as she confirms I am awake and conscious, and her arms come flying around my neck. I can feel the warmth of her fingertips heating my skin. I smile into her shoulder gratefully as she hugs me tighter. She feels familiar. She feels like home.

"What happened?" I croak out. I haven't spoken in a while, that's obvious, and I have no idea what's happened or how long I have been out. Sophie pulls away, moving so that she is perching on the side of the table that is closer to me. I look down and realize I am lying on a table myself, padded by a wad of blankets. When I look back at Sophie, she nervously flips her hair over her shoulder and something in the pit of my stomach tells me that it is bad.

"*Oh god*, what?"

"It's bad, Kay. It's so bad," she whispers.

I frown and try to shift my position so I can see her better but everything aches. "What do you mean?"

"Right," she starts, "it started after we went to sleep..."

"*I'll sleep on the floor,*" *I offer. The blankets Adam has dug out for us were decent and warm enough, and I feel so exhausted from today that I am craving sleep.*

"*If you're sure,*" *Damon says reluctantly and puts his stuff over two of the waiting chairs and eyes me with caution.*

"*I'm sure.*"

"*Okay, well, I guess good night.*" *Tom smiles at all of us and slips down next to Sophie, who is slumped against one of the chairs and looks miserable.*

"*Night,*" *I say, wriggling to get comfy.*

I look at Sophie and frown. "I remember all of that. I don't get where this is going."

"Just *listen*, Kayla." She interrupts with a motherly telling off. "It was about three in the morning when all shit went to hell…"

A scream echoes. The sound of deafening shrieks as someone struggles. I'm thrust awake, but I can't see. I can't see anything. But I can hear everything.

"The storm," someone screams. I can hear the windows shattering and more screams engulf the waiting room. The sounds of heavy footsteps and running pound past me but I'm paralyzed. I want to scream but I can't. My body is shaking. I manage to blink through the darkness and catch sight of a wad of glass sticking up through my thigh. There is blood everywhere; it's streaming out of my leg like a never-ending waterfall, splashing onto the floor. And then I can suddenly feel it—the pain is crippling.

But the storm is worse. It rips through the waiting room, tugging loose wood free and devastating everything in sight. My body won't move, and the sudden sensation of knowing that I'm going to die—this is it—makes me freeze. My body is turning to ice. And it's freezing. Fucking freezing.

Sophie stutters. "Evan, he…he saw you and you were having a fit, Kayla. On the floor with a massive shard of glass poking out of your thigh. It was so scary. He got you up and began running towards the double doors with the rest of us that were scrambling to get out," she explains. "You just kept having a fit. Your body felt so, so cold, but you also had a fever that Adam said was completely sky high. He said it caused you to go into complete shock."

"Put her on the counter!" It's Adam's voice, I recognize it. "Someone get me a damp cloth and a blanket," he orders.

Hands are suddenly touching my face. "Hold on," Adam whispers into my ear. "Just hold on really tight for me, okay? We will get this under control." And then, "Where the hell is the cloth at?"

Sophie shivers as she thinks back. "There was blood *everywhere*. The shard had cut through at least three veins and trapped a nerve. Adam said that the pain you must have been in and the sudden panic attack of not being able to move was a sign that you had gone into shock. The fit was a result of it." Sophie's voice fluctuates. "Adam asked us all to help..."

"Evan, untie your belt and tie it above the glass on her thigh; we need to stop it from bleeding. Sophie, hold her hand. Kayla's in shock, so she looks still, but the pain is most likely unbearable."

A cough.

"Damon, I need you to keep my briefcase open and hand me the exact things I need, alright? And Tom, mate, you really need to hold tightly onto that glass shard. I need to get it out, but I also need to make sure it doesn't hit any major ligaments, I can't see the damage from here." The sound of wind whirling and things breaking from a distance is evident, but I can't concentrate on anything other than the pain.

"So anyway, Adam got the shard out, but it was so scary because you didn't move once, Kayla. I thought you were dead." She reaches out to squeeze my hand. "But then the fits kept getting worse and it was like having to restrain an animal or something because Adam said we had to stop you from hurting yourself even more."

"Oh, my god." I breathe. The air feels trapped in my lungs. I don't remember.

"This kitchen had basic first aid kit, but nothing that could help you. You needed morphine—hell, you needed a hospital, but the best we had was the travel kit Adam had with him and the poxy first aid kit that was already in the kitchen," she makes a face and looks away. "But finally, the bleeding stopped, and Adam was ranting medical terms left, right and center as he stitched you up as best he could with thread from my jumper and a sterilized needle."

"I don't know if it was the pain or the shock or whatever, but your eyes closed, and it just looked as if you had fallen asleep. You were unconscious, for *three* days. You've been lying on this counter for three days."

My mouth opens, and I shudder. "But..."

"Adam said you haven't had another fit, which is good. He thinks that the coma helped stop them. But outside this room Kayla, it's so bad. The waiting room is torn to bits; there is no more duty-free, I mean very little of it and the storm has wrecked any form of a road that leads out of this place. At least the wind has stopped; it's just the rain, that's constant."

"Hey, hey, hey." I stop her. She's crying now. "It's okay, I'm okay. We are going to be okay." I reassure her, but I haven't got the faintest clue about what's happened outside of this room.

She wipes her face and shakes her head. "But that's not even the worst part."

"What are you talking about?"

"Ben and Jess," Sophie spits. "They have been cooped up in this kitchen the *whole* time."

"They have been here the whole time?" I gulp in a large mouthful of stale air and let my own tears roll down my cheeks. "They've been only three meters away this entire time?"

"Yeah," she says solemnly. "The whole time."

"I don't…I *can't.*" My lip quivers and it hits me. Like the storm hits my chest and the rain becomes my tears. It hits me everywhere. Right from the tips of my fingers to my toes. Benjamin Moore officially tore out my heart and hung it on the washing line to dry.

"I want to see him," I demand.

"No, Kayla," Sophie shakes her head, "that's probably not the best idea right now."

"No, Soph. I can't take this. I can't take feeling like this. I have to see him. I have to know why."

"I need to see you too." And there *he* is, standing at the door looking fresh-faced and frustratingly gorgeous just like every single time I have ever laid eyes on him.

"Maybe I should leave you to it then." Sophie stands hesitantly, but I catch her hand just in time.

"No." I shoot daggers at Ben. "This is definitely not going to take long."

"Kayla—" He steps forward, but something inside me snaps. I don't care about his reasons anymore. I'm angry. Hell, I'm pissed.

"I don't want to hear it. I don't want to hear another lie or another excuse. I don't want to know if you love *her*. Or if after you have been kissing me, you were swapping spit with her. I don't want to listen. I don't want to hear any of it. I am completely ashamed of myself for caring so deeply about some seventeen-year-old guy that clearly has too much fun getting it out to every girl. So, here's the 411: piss off. I don't want to see you, I don't want to look at you and I certainly don't want to think about you with *her*." I struggle to sit up. "And before you leave, if it wasn't obvious, you're dumped, you utter asshole."

Enraged, I force myself up properly and pant deeply, my breath catching up with me. I ignore the pain that follows by gritting my teeth and I don't look back up to see if Ben has left. I just know he's gone by Sophie's reaction.

"Damn girl." She smirks. "He certainly got what was coming to him."

Chapter Eight

I must have fallen asleep again because my head feels heavy when I wake up. The room smells of soap, the lemon kind that reminds you of detergent and of home. I blink mindlessly, focusing back on a figure beside me—Adam. He's got a thin needle in his hand and is trying to stick it into a small jar of something...

It takes me a moment to focus on what it is.

Morphine.

"Where did you get that?" I cough out every syllable, so I'm not even sure if he heard me. He spins around, his green eyes peering at me with a worried frown. He looks exhausted. Dark bags cloud under his eyes and I can tell from the number of times he blinks that he is trying to keep himself awake.

He forces a smile. "Rise and shine, you."

He starts to lightly shake the bottle of morphine. "So, it turns out that the first aid kit was found conveniently under the sink, and it had this baby in it. I'm not a hundred percent sure this is the real deal, but it's worth the risk."

I pull a face. "So, my life is literally in the hands of a vial of *could-be* morphine?" I try to pull myself upright and it takes a couple of attempts. I feel like my entire body is heavy as if it's been weighed down. My leg feels numb and I groan as I try to move them.

"Yeah." Adam laughs. "Basically."

I try to smile back at him, but my back aches from lying down for so long and my neck is stiff and rigid.

"How's the pain?" He asks worriedly.

"On a scale of one to ten, then right now is about a seven." My eyes drift onto a piece of glass the size of my hand, covered in blood and lying on the kitchen worktop. "*God*, what is that?"

"That wasn't…" I trail off because I already know the answer. *It was in my leg.*

"Well, it was poking out of your leg," Adam says as if he can read my mind.

"Oh my god."

"It's healing well," he explains, sitting on the edge of the table. He's changed since the last time I saw him and is wearing a plain black t-shirt that has a pocket on the right side. I notice a pile of dirty clothing beside the shard and can't stop the feeling of guilt that crawls through my body for getting blood on his clothes.

"The morphine has helped loads and the fact that your brain has been slipping into unconsciousness isn't ideal but seems to have stopped the swelling."

"Oh," I say because nothing else feels right. Silence engulfs the room, but I can't stop looking at him.

Adam blinks twice, his mouth twitching as if he is itching to say something. He's still fiddling with the needle and morphine.

"What is it?" I ask slowly.

"Hmm?"

"What are you desperate to say?" I repeat.

He blushes from being caught out. It's only slight, but I catch it. "Nothing," he says shortly but later adds, "it's none of my business, I mean

I barely even *know* you." He emphasizes what he says, and it sounds like it's more important from his accent.

I roll my eyes. "Adam, just spit it out already."

"I heard that your boyfriend cheated on you and I was just gonna say—"

"Kayla!" Damon bursts through the room, arms wide and a bunch of something chocolaty under his arm. Three steps forward, then he reaches for me and wraps his arms around my neck. My back hurts with the strain. I make an effort to hug him back, but he pulls away soon after and I'm relieved.

"How are you?"

"I'm…" I trail off. "Fine."

He smirks. "Liar."

"Yeah, well, I'm being optimistic," I reply, gruffly.

"You don't need to be optimistic, Kayla," Damon says carefully. "You've been through a lot. You're alive."

I smile. "So have you guys."

He shrugs. "That's different and you know it."

"I suppose," I agree reluctantly. I chew the inside of my lip as I try to sit up straighter and can feel the pain getting worse. Adam fiddles with the morphine more until he gives me a look and I know relief is coming.

•　　•　　•

It's late by the time Adam gives me the *go signal* to move. I get Damon to fill me in on the recent goings-on, but he mostly just talks about the weather. He tells me it's been calm, that the worst seems to be over but that in no way does that mean we are able to leave just yet. He also talks about Ben and Jess and that they now have come completely come out of hiding. It's that evening when I see her that I can't think of anything else but what she has done, and not just to me, but to Evan.

I'm not sure what on earth I am doing until I'm sitting down next to her, limping from my injury. My legs feel useless, heavy, and they pull behind me and won't listen to where I want them to go. Once I manage to sit, I think I have nothing to say, but I know I could throw several choice phrases at her. Jess catches my eye as I sit, and I can almost feel the wariness radiating off her body.

"Kayla," she starts uncertainly. "I just want to say that I really am sorry. I honestly didn't want to come between you and Ben, and I really didn't want you to find out like this either."

"I don't care." I stop her.

She blinks suddenly. "Wait, what?"

"I said that I don't care, Jess. In fact, the whole ordeal is driving me mad and not in the way you're thinking. Yes, you did a shitty thing. Yes, I got hurt. But I'm over it, or at least I am trying to be. This isn't why I'm here." I tell her.

She faces me properly and frowns. "You're not?"

"No, Jess." I shrug my shoulders but almost instantly regret it. "I'm here because despite disliking both Evan and you for as long as I've known, I have come to realize that if anything can come out of this, it is that you need to sort your shit out and stop leading Evan on. He's…an *okay* guy, and by never putting an end to these rumors about your apparent 'relationship,' you are putting ideas in his head and hurting him more."

"I don't know what you're talking about, Kayla." She makes a face as if to say the idea is ridiculous. I fumble with the cuff of my sleeve, anxious as to whether this is my place to mention anything or not. I know Evan and I aren't exactly friends, but the kid helped save my life, so I owe him this much.

"Oh, common, Jess, the guy is pretty much in love with you."

Jess puckers a brow, taking it all in, and then laughs. *Really* loud.

"You've got to be kidding me." She disregards my words. "I've known Evan for years. It's *always* been platonic. You really don't have a clue, do you?"

"Then why did you never tell anyone otherwise?" I ask, puzzled by her reply. "Plenty of people have asked you."

"Where's the fun in that?" She smirks as if it's always been a game. I can't help but grimace.

"So, you're telling me it's fun to mess with people's feelings?"

She takes a second to reply, and when she does, I can't tell if she's joking or not. "Evan doesn't really have feelings." I just stare at her. Evan might be a dick, but he's not emotionless. She sighs and adds, "Like he doesn't *feel* things the way other people do."

"So, you're saying he's a psychopath?"

She chuckles and shakes her head. "I'm saying that Evan has been taught to be void of any emotion. Life hasn't been good to him at home, so he's learned not to care. His barriers are so far up I don't think anyone will get through. He's never cared much about anything, and that's fine until you can't stop yourself from caring about him." She shuffles on the chair and I know she doesn't like where this conversation is going.

Jess fiddles with her hands and shrugs. "There was a time I cared for Evan, like a lot, but I could never figure out with him if the feelings were reciprocated."

"I just…" I lose myself in my thoughts just as I catch Evan walking back into the room with Sophie alongside him. Something stirs in my stomach, a weird feeling and for a second, I look at the boy as if this is the first time I have seen him. "Just make sure that when you tell him, you let him down gently. The guy isn't as tough and 'void of emotion' as you make him out to be," I add using air quotes.

Jess smiles and it looks genuine. "Yeah," she agrees. "He deserves that."

"Brilliant news, guys." Sophie and Evan appear in front of us. I cringe, hoping they haven't heard what we said. "We found the guards."

"And?" Jess butts in before I can answer.

"And they think we're gonna be out of here by tomorrow."

Chapter Nine

"And people say that school vacations are boring." Evan sneers beside me. The police car rattles against the cobbled pavements that cover the streets of Rome. I'm soaked in an unfamiliar liquid, and I'm even more convinced that I have peed a little as the cop fastened my handcuffs moments earlier. The frustration of trying to decipher the cop's bad English as he read me my rights makes me question if I need a lawyer or not. And I'm pissed, again, which happens a lot recently when Evan Winters is involved.

"We have just been arrested, Evan!" I cry. "I'd hardly call this the kickstart to the weekend trip we'd finally started getting," I say bitterly. The taste of the lemon spritzer he had made me down earlier is just as bitter in my throat.

"It was hardly *my* fault," he says defensively, swinging one leg over the other. "You're the demented one who thought bargaining a chicken for some *'soldi soldi'* was a good idea." Soldi being money. I want to kick him. It *wasn't* even my suggestion. This entire elaborate plot was concocted by him.

"Oh, for God's sake, the chickens weren't even my idea!" The furious look I have been armed with since the police tossed us into this car suddenly fades and I realize something. "Holy shit, we are going to *jail.*"

"Well…" Evan leers, the muddy water he had face planted into on the way here is now sticking chunks of his hair together. "It could be worse."

I look at him, bewildered. "Really, how might that be?"

"We could've actually sold the man that chicken." He's laughing before he finishes his sentence and before I have a chance to smack him.

My bewilderment turns to disbelief. "It's *not* funny, Winters."

"Don't do that." He cuts off his laughter with a cough.

"Do what?"

"Use my last name as if it's meant to evoke some sort of authority," he says numbly. I realize this is a case of déjà vu. Expressionless, he proceeds to fiddle with his seat belt. "You sound like my *dad.*"

"I use it because the way Evan sounds is just *so*…oh, forget it, I don't want to talk to you." I turn away as best I can and face the window. The police car stops, one of the policemen went out to greet the chicken man who stands with his eyes wide at the front steps of the police station. I watch him express his anger through wild gestures, giggling into my sleeve as he uses the middle finger and waves it at the two of us.

"You're going to have to talk to me eventually, Kayla." Evan sighs and leans back against the leather seat. "It looks like we're taking the high road together."

"Over my dead body," I mutter.

I can hear Evan chuckle. "It's not going to be just your dead body you're gonna be worried about when we are confined within four walls." His handcuffs clink against the window. "It's gonna be both of ours."

3 days earlier…

It all happened so fast.

One moment I'm trapped in a torrential storm with a neighbor I have hated for years and a handful of non-English speaking tourists, and the next, six preened guards file through the duty-free area with smiling faces and with the news that the weather warning that has now been lifted to a category safe for us to evacuate.

"It's happening," Sophie murmurs, clapping her hands together like we are waiting for the arrival of someone's kid. "We're finally getting out of this place."

"I'm just dying to ask where the hell they have been for this past week," I say sourly. Sophie raises her eyebrows, agreeing. I am too busy looking at her that I miss it at first. It's a glare—the kind that could be easily mistaken for lighting. It flashes in my eyes a second time, and this time Sophie notices it too.

"What is that?" I ask, putting my hand over my face to shield my eyes.

"The second coming," Sophie says amusedly and I smack her arm, wobbling as my bad leg still isn't strong yet.

She walks towards the window, her shoes crunching on the leftover glass. She gasps, and I follow her to the window where she tugs at my arm and points to the other building. I don't see anything.

"I can't see anything, Soph," I say out loud.

"Come here, *look,*" she replies, sounding agitated.

But just as I step back to where she is standing, the flash comes again, and I squint enough to see someone standing at a window, something reflective in their hand—a mirror. I have to squint more, and that's when I see it, her swishing bob. I think it's Mrs. Scott.

"It's a signal. They know we are here," Sophie says what we are both thinking.

"What happened?" I make a face. The last thing we had discussed as a group was for us to try and find a way of getting to them.

"We couldn't help, Kayla." Sophie busts her elbow through the crack in the glass and it shatters at our feet. I'm not sure what her plan is exactly. I can feel the sudden gust of wind reach through the holes in my t-shirt and I wrap my arms around myself.

Sophie bends down to the broken glass. "The storm got so bad that as soon as we would have stepped out there, we'd have been killed."

I only nod because I wasn't there to see it, but the devastation it's caused doesn't leave me second guessing. I watch as she picks up the largest piece of glass from the floor and stares up towards the sky. "Move," she commands. "I need good light."

I do as she says and Sophie fiddles with the glass in her palm to get it just right, holding it up and catching a glare from the sun that seeps through the clouds, waving it towards the outer building. It takes a moment, but the glass reflects back onto the building and she is signaling back to our class.

"Signal received." She looks proud of herself.

"Where on earth did you learn to do that?" I ask her.

"I listen in class." She drops the piece of glass and unpicks some of the shards that stick into her palm with a flick of her finger. "And summer camp."

"I didn't even know you went to summer camp," I say.

"Not here," she explains. "In England. It was this survival camp thing when I was twelve. Boring as hell, but there were some really cute boys."

I laugh. "You were twelve."

"I was old enough."

"You're gross."

She grins. "And you love it."

•   •   •

It is 10:30 by the time the airport security translates what is happening. Adam recites the plan to a small group of us who didn't hear. It is simple: single formation, three double-decker coaches for our building, two for the outer one. We will be taken first to the hospital to be treated for any injuries we may have and then to an undamaged refugee hotel that has been compensated by the Italian government. It's not ideal, but it's better than what we've been used to.

"When do we leave?" I ask him. Adam runs his fingers through his hair. He's stressed, I can feel it. I feel tense around him as well. I have been desperate to speak to him for days, but he's been too busy. I want to thank him for saving my life, for helping me.

"In ten minutes," he informs me, letting his shoulders sag a bit. "I really need to get to a phone."

"Why?" Though it's a stupid question; we all want to call home. I think about Mom and everyone at home and my heart stings. She must be completely freaking out.

"I'm meant to be here as part of my medical training for the army." Adam's voice is distant, worried. "I haven't made contact."

"I'm sure they would've heard," I try to reassure him. "It's probably been all over the news."

He looks skeptical. "But what if it hasn't?" But we both know it has, he's overthinking it.

"Then all you can do is explain. At the end of the day, it's not your fault, Adam." I touch his arm in the hope it brings some sort of comfort to him. With his free hand, he brushes my knuckles, and my breath catches.

"Thank you," I say, feeling more inclined to show my gratefulness.

"For what?" His eyebrows furrow.

"For saving my life, for doing all of this. This place wouldn't have survived if it wasn't for you." I conclude. My leg is strapped up and is healing and it wouldn't be in the state it is now if Adam hadn't helped me. My fingers lace through his and instead of breaking apart, he pulls me closer to him steadily, wrapping his arms around my waist and looping them together. His hug is warm, soft, and he smells of pine wood and leaves. It is a comfort I have needed, and it surprises me how much one simple hug can make me feel a thousand times better.

"Are you coming to the refugee hotel?" I question, pulling away. I regret it, my body feeling cold without his warmth.

"For a little while," Adam says, but he sounds reluctant and I am not going to lie and say it doesn't bother me. "I will be there just until I can make contact and get further instructions."

"Right, of course." I'm being silly. He has a job to do—an *important* one. But it isn't what I want to hear. Adam smiles his goodbye for the moment and leaves me. In three long strides, Evan grabs my wrist and pulls me towards the wall, talking in a low voice. I notice he's careful about my leg and it makes me smirk in wonder, the boy can be alright sometimes.

"It looks like we're finally getting out of this place," he says.

"Looks like it," I whisper.

"Why are you whispering?" Evan smirks at me and drops my wrist.

"Why are you?"

"I need a beer," he speaks loudly, making a point. He gets a few funny looks.

"I need a bath, a nice, hot, bubbly one." I fantasize about it. I can't remember the last time I washed properly without having to splash some freezing cold water under my arms.

"Anything hot would be great right now." Evan smiles and peers outside the window. "Hey, look, they're here."

The coaches roll up alongside a couple of vans with rescue teams in them. Evan drops his hand from the window and it swings next to his side but not before his fingers catch mine. It's only for a moment, maybe even less than that, but I feel electricity surge through me. I dismiss it as the feeling of getting out, of finally escaping.

Yes, it's definitely that.

Chapter Ten

2 days earlier…

"In other news, headline weather reports state that the storm that overtook Italy's capital for the past week has left mass destruction in its wake. Emergency services have been swamped with calls from citizens and tourists alike, all stuck in the storm. The death toll is currently at twelve people, four of those being children. Considering these events, Italy's government has reached out in hope for aid…"

It's the same story, repeated on the news again and again and *again*. We've been on the coach for all of half an hour and the radio crackles with the same report each time. Somehow Mrs. Scott has managed to gain some cell reception from somewhere despite most of the major towers being down and is now keeping us updated from reports from CBS and Fox News which apparently our class is all over.

"We're famous," Damon says from the seat behind me. He is sitting with Evan, who hasn't spoken a word the entire journey until now.

"We're not famous Damon," he snaps at his friend. "Shut up."

Sophie peers over the seats and gives Evan a nasty look. "No need to throw your toys out of the pram just because Damon's excited about something after the shitty week we've had."

Evan narrows his eyes at her. "You didn't hear me asking for your opinion anywhere in there, did you?"

Sophie rolls her eyes and Damon raises an eyebrow. "That's enough, Evan."

Sophie, monumentally pissed, turns back around and grunts. I reach over and squeeze her hand. "Ignore him," I say loud enough for Evan to hear. "He's a particular ass when he's hungry."

Sophie giggles and turns to peer out of the window. The chaos and destruction that has been left behind are astronomical. Roofs have been torn off houses and buildings, cars are stacked on top of each other, pieces of wood and metal are sticking up from stacks of rubble. The more I look the worse I see.

"It's so awful," Sophie murmurs as she fiddles with a piece of loose string from her sweater. "We are lucky to be alive."

"I don't even know how we are," I agree numbly, my eyes diverting from the wreckage and instead to the geometrically patterned seat in front of me, particularly ugly but better than looking at the devastation out of the window.

"Fate," Damon intervenes from behind again, "or luck, but either way don't sit and question it. Karma isn't what you want right now."

We drive past what looks like a school. Most of the left side of it has been crushed by a broken building from behind and a wall of flowers beside the gate flutter in the wind with pictures of missing or dead children. I can't tell. The cold chill that cascades down my back puts me on edge and my heart stings.

"Those kids . . . imagine how scared they must have been." Sophie shakes her shoulders as the same feeling runs through her as well. "There is bound to be more deaths, but where do you even start looking?" She's barely audible, her voice void of happiness. I don't want to think about it. I *can't*. It's too much. It's not fair, and it's definitely not right. I turn in my seat and look through the peephole. I watch Evan look down to his wrist where a threaded bracelet his sister Chelsea gave him rests, and I know he is worried about her. My brother Cameron and Evan's sister are in the same class and are actually friends despite their older siblings. I think about my brother, and his bright blonde hair and I can't wait to be home even more. I need that little boy like I need air. I just haven't realized how much until now.

I try to close my eyes and listen to the conversations around me. The radio cycles the same story once more, the same script reciting the same thing. I have heard it so many times that I hear myself whispering the words as she says them. I pull the sweater I have been given tighter over my shoulders, pulling my legs up to my chin so that nobody can see the tears that wet my cheeks. And all I can think about is the kids, just the kids. I think about how they will never learn to ride a bike or ever get married or start a family. I think about everything they have lost and think about how much left I have to do, how I am lucky to be doing any of it.

So, I make myself a pact. It won't be for me, it will be for them.

•   •   •

It's hot, and it drizzles. It smooths out my hair and warms my neck. It ripples over my shoulders and cascades continuously in heaps over my bare skin. I lean my head back in the shower, standing there for a moment and letting the water wash away the last week. The refugee hotel is large, satisfyingly fitting all of us and other vacationers who have been caught in the storm. It's nothing special but includes hot water, a bed, and food. And all of that is a luxury I didn't know I would have again.

Once the water starts to run cold, I step out of the shower and grab a towel sitting on top of the toilet seat as quickly as I can, wrapping it around my body in hope for quick warmth. My wet hair cools my hot back as I tuck the flyways behind my ear and stare at myself in the small mirror above the sink. For once in what feels like forever, I feel clean.

I don't know what it is about showers, but they are great for washing away the shit you don't want to think about. Like the last week or an argument with your mom or dad or a crap grade on a project. They're great until you step out of them and suddenly there is nothing washing away the shit anymore. It's just you and the problem.

I'm looking at myself and I look different. My hair is still the same shade of boring brown and my eyes are still dark and grey. I'm still five foot two and never growing taller, but the more I stare at myself, the more I can see something has changed. The way I carry myself? My healing leg? I can't put my finger on it.

I drop my gaze and grab the end of the towel and squeeze the water out of my hair just as a voice looms near the door.

"I just need to use the bathroom."

I freeze as the door rattles and bursts open. I don't have a second to think about what to do next because Evan has appeared in the doorway.

"Um…"

"Oh," his cheeks flush, and I can't believe he looks embarrassed; I'm the one standing naked in a towel.

"Err…"

"*Oh.*"

"Get out!" I find my voice. Evan blinks rapidly, snapping him out of his stare, and stumbles back out, holding his hands out in surrender. I huff, sticking my leg out to kick the door close. I can hear a sudden high-pitched laugh—*Sophie's*—and then the sound of the TV blaring. At least she finds this amusing. I can't help but think despite their tiff on the coach ride here, they have been awfully close recently. I pull on some clothes all borrowed from Sophie as my suitcase has not arrived yet, but I am still cold so I pull back on the sweater I was given and open the door.

"I don't think you should bring it up," Sophie speaks, her voice on edge. "She's already been through enough."

"But she deserves to know," this time Evan speaks, a flicker of concern laced with his words. I am about to walk in, asking them to enlighten me on what they are talking about. But I don't, I already know, or I have a pretty good guess.

"She may deserve to know, but this is going to *kill her*. Could you imagine finding out that your boyfriend had lied to you about his virginity and instead slept with someone the day before you both did?" Sophie's voice is hard; she's angry. I don't need to hear a name; she's talking about Ben—what Ben did to me.

And there it is.

The last stab of the knife. It's the pain you get after you hit your funny bone, or the insignificance you feel when a rejection letter from your favorite college sits at your front door.

Disgusted with both myself and him, for being blind to his lies this entire time, I grab the room key from the side of the vanity and storm out of the hotel room, my leg dragging like dead weight behind me. I was given crutches when we visited the hospital, along with a bunch of pain meds and a proper dressing for my wound, but I leave them all behind even though each step I take wails at me to turn around. The tears splash down my cheeks the faster I walk, and I can taste the salt on my lips by the time Sophie has realized it is me who has stormed off and is calling my name. The elevator doors open, and I can hear her footsteps running after me as she tries to get my attention. I know it's not her fault, but I want to be alone. I know she must hate herself right now, but I can't do with making her feel better when I can't even help myself.

The doors of the elevator begin to close, and I have to squeeze in quickly, trapping not only myself but the overwhelming emotion that I'm not good enough. And it's shit. At the end of the day the realization that I *have never* been good enough is sufficient to make me cry harder. I look back at the last three years I have spent with Ben Moore and come to the inevitable conclusion: it was a lie. The whole fucking thing. Every single word, emotion, and act was *false*. I have been living a lie and everyone knew it. Evan *knew* it.

I slump to the floor, the tears pouring down my cheeks like angry waterfalls, pooling on my chin. I want to scream, but I can't even open my mouth. The elevator doesn't move, so I shakily stand, pressing a random button. I don't even realize that the doors have opened again until someone speaks.

"Come on," a voice murmurs. "I know something that will help." I look up in time for him to press the ground floor button. It's Adam. And I don't know whether to be flattered he wants to make me feel better or embarrassed he has seen me like this. I decide the former. And I collapse into his open arms.

Chapter Eleven

1 day earlier…

Adam's idea is ice cream, which is definitely not what I am expecting considering the state of things outside of the hotel. However, we do a couple of laps around the hotel before standing outside the ice cream store across the street. It's closed, obviously.

I'm not really sure what he was expecting.

"Well, uh…that sucks." Adam furrows his eyebrows after rattling on the door a couple of times in case someone was indeed inside. He bends down and produces a key tucked under the mat of the store and winks.

"Wow," I mumble and fold my arms. "Italy is very trusting."

Adam smiles, slipping the key into the lock and twisting it. I know it's wrong; this is someone's business, someone's income. We're breaking and entering. I want to turn back around and say, *forget it, we can just carry on walking,* but Adam fishes out his wallet and sticks twenty euros on the counter, already paying for our ice creams, and I feel a little better. I guess we used the key, so maybe breaking and entering is a little extreme.

"So which flavor?" he asks, slipping a large ice cream cone off the pile and grabbing a spoon. The lights aren't on, and I can't read the labels on the ice cream because they're in Italian, but I manage to pick both flavors that resemble chocolate brownie and caramel fudge.

"Good choice." Adam compliments and hands me the cone.

"So what about you?" I scan the flavors, hoping to guess his choice. The store is small, with a single counter and a small array of diner-style chairs and tables. Posters from bands and businesses decorate the walls, coinciding with the menu. The floor is marble and makes my dirty shoes stand out more predominantly.

"I've always been a mint guy myself," Adam says, picking up another cone and spoons a large helping of mint ice cream into his cone.

"Oh, you have?" I raise an eyebrow; mint isn't a popular ice cream choice back at my house. "Only mint?" I try to not sound judgmental.

He grins and gives me a little wink as he sticks the spoon into the tub of water. "Yeah. It's pretty much the best flavor, both refreshing and chocolaty at the same time."

I giggle. "Thank you for that description."

"You're very welcome." He starts to lick at the corner of his melting cone, the green mint flavor trickling down the sides.

Adam swings the keys in his hand and we walk out of the store. He locks the door and places the key back under the mat. We walk in silence for a moment, our feet heading in the opposite direction of the hotel and I try to rack my brain for something to say. I know I look a mess, my hair is wet still from my shower and my eyes are raw and puffed up. I know this isn't a date or means anything more than a guy trying to cheer me up through ice cream, but I can't help myself wondering what it could be. Dangerous thinking coming from a girl who has just got out of something with a shitty boy. And maybe that's the thing, Adam's not a boy; he's older. He's a man.

Once we turn the corner of the road, I ask him, "So, what's it like?"

"What's what like?" He glances at me through his thick lashes.

"The army, what's it like?" I don't know if I'm treading on risky ground. I don't know if this is going to bring back bad memories he doesn't want to relive or get him into any kind of trouble by breaking some national security code or something. He's been weird about talking about it since I met him, which makes me think something has happened that he doesn't want to speak about.

He looks straight ahead, his shoulders slumping, and shrugs. "It's the best and the worst experience you'll ever have. It's the friends you make and the bonds you share with people, the respect you gain that make all the bad, all the killing somewhat bearable…" He trails off and licks at his ice cream. "I mean I don't see much action at the moment. I'm kinda just here to pick up the pieces."

"Yeah, that's what I was going to ask, what made you want to go into medicine?" I smile at him and catch the drips of ice cream that fall onto my hand.

"I spent almost a year in Afghanistan with my unit on the field. It was rough, mostly quiet, but it felt like you were always waiting for the penny to drop if you get what I mean?" He looks at me and shakes his head and continues.

"Nearly every other day I heard that another friend I had made had been killed or severely injured. I joined the army because I wanted to help my country; it is something that has been passed down through my family for generations. It was just simply my turn. But those reports soon became every single day and I knew I couldn't just sit and do nothing."

"About a year ago, I was driving through a patch of really flat desert land. I knew it was risky, we were completely exposed, but this was the route we had to take. We ended up on minefields. And suddenly I'm thrown five meters into the air and I wake up in a grimy room with news that my entire unit had been killed."

"You were the only one who survived?" I say with a gasp.

Adam nods. "I still had eight broken bones, been unconscious for almost two weeks, and have an impressive scar on my back now to prove it. It was just one of those moments where I couldn't breathe. I was devastated, crushed. They were all my brothers, they were my family and they got completely wiped out. It took around six months for me to recover, and I just decided then that my tour was done, and I'd come back this time helping my brothers, my team. I joined medical."

I grab his hand and squeeze. "You're the bravest person I've ever met," I tell him and look down at our joined hands. "I don't know how you do it."

I close the distance between us, pulling a strand of hair from his face. His lips meet mine before I have the chance. *It's okay.* This kiss says. *You are going to be okay.* And for the first time since we arrived, I believe it.

•   •   •

When we reach the hotel, Adam promptly leaves as a note lets him know his unit chief has called. I'm still reeling from the kiss, every step lighter than before. My leg doesn't feel so much like dead weight and I'm so giddy I keep knocking into things. I had allowed myself to forget for a minute where I was, what this all means. Out there it was just Adam and I but being back here sends an almost breath stopping reminder that somewhere here Ben is lurking around.

To my surprise, I am shocked to learn that this hotel has a pool after grabbing a leaflet from the front desk. The leaflet is mostly in Italian besides a couple of words, and if it wasn't for everything going on outside, it's pictured to be the beautiful in-town resort for miles. I think about being here if this was any other day but today, any other time, any other year and what it would be like, who would be beside me. If this storm never happened, would I be here right now?

I find the pool and see the covering has been ripped from it, mud and grass and other bits and pieces have been tossed into the water, but nothing that looks too dangerous. I lean down and run my hand through the water and it's warm, heated so I dangle my feet in and just sit.

"You're either in deep thought or constipated."

I look up, alarmed. Evan towers above me, a smirk placed on his lips like it is built there for him. His expression is a lot like this around me and I know he does it out of some weird kind of enjoyment, torment more like.

"You either have one facial expression, or you save all your smirks for me," I fire back, swishing my legs in the water. Evan sits beside me, dipping his own legs in. I look down and notice he has bruising all up on the side, but they are mostly discolored now and yellow, so I'm not sure if he got them whilst he was here or before.

"It's only you, baby," he teases and licks his lips dramatically.

I splash him. "You're unbelievable."

"Coming from you."

"Whatever."

I don't have anything to say to him, and the silence is becoming awkward. I wish he would just leave me in my mood. The giddy feeling I experienced earlier has vanished and instead, I feel cold and sad, *moody*. My mind focuses back to what Sophie had said in the room and it only worsens my mood. I don't know why Evan's here or why he isn't saying anything or why he even thinks this is just normal for us to be sitting here in silence together until I catch him fiddling nervously with his hands. He avoids eye contact when he starts to speak.

"So about earlier…"

"I don't want to talk about it," I snap sharply but I can feel my eyes pool again and I squeeze them shut to stop myself from crying any more than I have done.

"Yeah, you do," he murmurs. "Kayla, I would be feeling just as crap as you do right now."

"Not helping, Evan."

"My point is that we... *I* didn't want you to find out like that. It wasn't fair, and we should've told you as soon as we found out. Ben is a colossal dickhead—"

"Evan it's okay. You don't have to do this, we aren't—"

"—friends?" He stares at me. "I know Kayla, but it's also my fault and it makes me feel weird knowing you're upset about it."

I look at him baffled. "And?"

"*And* it makes me angry. *He* makes me so angry."

I stare at him for the longest second and try to read his true intentions, but he looks sincerer than I have ever seen him. "I feel like..." I trail off, my words failing me. I feel so much I don't know how to form them into a proper sentence.

"It's okay," he reassures me. It's the second time I have heard it today, once from myself and now once from Evan, but both start to make it feel real.

I shake my head. I need to let it out. "I feel like I'm standing in a crowded room with thousands of people, and that I'm screaming but my voice is another click of a shoe or an opening of a door. I don't feel heard. I never have. I'm drowning. I'm flooded with lies and feelings that are all false, and that every single time I was told I was loved, I wasn't, and every kiss was just cementing more and more lies. I feel worthless. I feel...*fake*." My head is spinning but steadily slows down as Evan's arms loop over my shoulder and he pulls me to his chest.

I can feel his own head lower and he kisses the top of my head. It's something I have seen him do with his little sister thousands of times before and makes me feel unsteady that he's doing the same with me. This is weird; we have never touched before, and not like this. Hugging isn't something we were accustomed to, it hasn't been for years, but I don't want to pull away.

"Sometimes the choices we make in life are the ones that hurt others the most. But it's not how the choices affect others; it's how they affect you. If you think of life as a tightrope, wobbly at the start, but in the middle, there's a stretch of rope that's not wobbly at all. What I'm saying is that life is one ongoing ride, but the ride eventually stops, and you have to get off. You won't feel like this forever Kayla, I promise you."

"But what if I do?" I whisper into his chest. My eyes are squeezed shut, but I can smell him and he smells good, really good.

"You won't. Besides, what did I tell you back at the airport?" I can feel him grinning on my head.

"I can't remember," I say honestly.

"You want revenge, right? Kick him where it hurts the most?" Evan asks, a lick of playfulness iced his voice.

"His dick?" I make a face. "It's not the type of pain I am going for but—"

"Kayla, it is a metaphor for what I really mean," he interrupts, laughing.

"Right, obviously," I say. "So, what's the plan?"

I pull away, ready. Evan winks, his face lighting up. "Well first, we need half a dozen chickens…"

Chapter Twelve

Evan only seems to have crappy ideas—ideas so bad that I know I will either end up dead, or worse, in jail.

The boy is baffling. I don't know how he thinks this is going to work. His plan increases in idiocy by the second; the more elaborate it gets, the more I know I shouldn't go along with it. But I've also never seen someone so excited about something. He speaks so enthusiastically and passionately about his plan that a part of me wants to do it for him because I know it will make him happy. The thought itself is as mystifying as I feel, and I shiver as if it's escaping from me.

The hotel has one computer occupied by the receptionist. I'm surprised to see that Evan, broody and silent, only have to waggle his eyebrows and smile for the receptionist to allow us to use it. The more I think about it, the more I consider the fact this can't be Evan's first rodeo. Most of the servers are down which means that every page takes a thousand years to load and I am growing bored of standing. My leg still aches, though a majority of the pain has subsided. I even try to point this out to Evan who, after my eighth complaint, pulls me down and onto his lap. I can only assume how this looks, but I am more thankful for the relief this gives me and decide to use him to my advantage. I grab the mouse out of Evan's hands and reload the page. It comes up almost instantly.

"How did you do that?" Evan leans over my arm, his lips so close to my skin that I shiver again. I know he feels it too, his body reacts in sync.

"Some talents can't be explained," I tell him, trying to ignore the way his breath tingles my skin. Evan's Google search is something to do with places to buy chickens. 3, 094 results appear; only two translated into English with the slow internet.

"This is going to be harder than I thought," Evan mutters as we read the page. He retakes the mouse from me and clicks aimlessly at it, highlighting the text and then unhighlighting it.

"Would you quit doing that?" I pull the mouse out of his hands again and I feel as if we're sitting here fighting over a toy or something. I lean to get control over the computer and type in 'local chicken farms' into Google and press search, hoping this will narrow down the results. It does, but the same problem presents itself.

"We need someone who can translate this," I say, my shoulders slumping slightly. "Why don't you go make yourself useful and ask one of the hotel staff?" I suggest.

"Why do I have to do it?" Evan complains, sounding like a five-year-old. "This was my master plan. You go do the shitty work."

"Yes, exactly, this is *your* idea, Evan." I sound nearly as pathetic as him. "That means you have to do it."

"Fine. Whatever." He stands up and pushes me up with him. I catch myself on the desk and watch as he stalks off and then sit back down, scrolling to the top of the page and wait.

He likes to take his time and I'm pretty sure he's doing it deliberately. When he does finally return, his brown hair bobbing back into view, he's brought a boy no older than thirteen who is dressed as if he's about to play a round of golf. I stare at his feet, which are the only thing out of place of his whole look. He is wearing flip-flops and I think he must have raided some kind of clothes bin to come up with this combo. The boy catches me looking and meets my eye, winking. I think I might vomit as they both reach us, Evan first, his long legs striding across the foyer.

"Jesus Christ Evan, why did you have to pick the prepubescent Italian?"

He shrugs, but he's smirking through it. "He can speak English," he says so casually, but we both know he could have picked just about anyone else. I grunt my reply and turn back to the computer.

"Don't complain." He smirks and beckons the boy over, mimicking me. "This is *your* idea."

The Italian boy smiles and steps forward, one eyebrow-raising suggestively. "What can I do for you, lady?"

"Save me," I whisper meekly.

•   •   •

The cab bumps across another pothole in the road, rattling every bone in my body. The leather seats that crumble beneath my fingertips are both disgusting and kind of radical, considering the thought of the hundreds of people who have taken their own journeys across Rome, making their own memories. Finding a cab between the chaos and havoc was hard enough, but somehow Evan managed to flag one down and I guess we have to be grateful for what we got. Speaking of the devil, he sits beside me with his phone in his hands; he keeps looking at it like he's expecting a call and I want to know who from.

"Just call them," I say, more forcefully than necessary.

"Sorry?" He blinks at me through those thick lashes of his.

"Whoever you're waiting to get a call from, make the move and call them," I repeat, trying to not sound nosey despite being desperate to know who he wants to speak to. Most phones aren't working with the cell reception down because of the storm. I haven't even spoken to my family yet.

"I don't want to while she's…doing it," he speaks aloud, though he directs it to the chair in front of him.

"Who's doing what?"

"Jess." He nervously chews on his bottom lip. "She is breaking up with Ben today."

"Wait, *what*?" I move my seatbelt so I can face him.

"Before I saw you yesterday, Jess came to my room and told me that it took talking to someone to realize her real feelings for me." He shrugs as I gulp, and I already know what he's about to say before it comes out of his mouth. "Kayla, she said she loved me."

"Oh, don't be ridiculous." The words tumble out of my mouth before I can stop it. I know it's far too harsh and he doesn't really deserve it, but the entire notion of it makes my stomach feel funny.

He turns to me and stares, disbelief fluttering over his features. "What?"

"I really didn't mean it like that." I cringe and turn to face him, the leather seat screeching as I do. "I mean come on . . . it's taken her now to realize this? When did she have this epiphany then, hmm? Whilst she's sleeping with Ben and every other guy back at home, or when she's busy rubbing all of that in your face? I'm sorry, I don't think so." I take a big gulp of air and slowly inhale it, trying to think of the best thing to do and say. I know I was the one she spoke to, I know I sparked this, but I didn't expect her to come back saying this.

Angry is an understatement, and Evan doesn't even try to hide it. His face is like thunder, each word I speak a slap in the face and the guilt starts to push up, but I force it down. He has to know.

"You're one to talk," he spits at me. I can see his eyes tear up and I know I've really hurt him which is why I try to stop what he says next from affecting me. "I wouldn't even expect you to understand. It's clear now: Ben never even liked you. I don't think you know what it's like to be in—"

"—in love? Jesus, Evan, I *have* been since I was fourteen." I'm shaking. "I can't believe you would ever say that. Friends or not, I just can't."

"We are friends, Kayla." He sighs like the anger just leaves like that.

But it doesn't come as easily to me. "Really, Evan, are you hearing yourself? She has never given one fuck about you at all, like ever. I've been on good terms with you for little over a week and I've been a better friend to you than she has in *six years*."

"I was going to say something." Evan lets out a sharp breath I hadn't noticed he had been holding in.

I snort. "Of course, you were."

"She loves me, Kayla. I know she does. She's going to be my girlfriend. She's going to make me happy." But he sounds as if he's trying to convince himself.

My anger subsides slightly, and I grab the cell phone from his hands and shake it in his face. "Love isn't trying to convince someone else you are the person who is going to make them happy. Love is seeing that you already are."

"Arrival," the taxi driver announces, pulling up to a shack with a crooked sign tied with rope to a broken lamppost.

"Oh right." I reach over and grab my wallet, shoving a couple of twenties in his hand. "Thank you."

We watch him drive away, and I face the chicken farm. "Evan…" I trail off. It's awkward now, and I hand him back his phone. "I'm—"

"It's fine, you're right," is all he mutters and looks down to the floor.

I try to focus on the plan. "So, what do we say? 'Excuse me. May we buy a dozen chickens?'"

Evan wraps an arm around my shoulder and squeezes. "Yeah." He begins to walk. "Exactly."

.   .   .

And suddenly it's all happening at once.

The courtyard is empty except for a few tourists slipping change into a busker's open guitar case. We're running, and my hair is soaking and sticky, the wind blowing tangled, wet strings of hair into my face. I can hear my laughter ringing, bouncing off the walls and consuming the air. My breath catches, and I trip against the cobbled pavements, falling into Evan who is just in front. He's grinning, the chicken cage still under his armpit, and pulls me upright, tugging on my arm to pull me forward. Maybe this isn't the best idea, but maybe I have known that all along.

Maybe I don't care.

Maybe it is all worth it.

"I feel so free," Evan yells, lifting his free arm into the air. His pace quickens as he sidesteps the guy singing and zooms down the side of the nearest building so that I can't see him. It doesn't take me long to catch up with him. I can feel my heartbeat with every thud my converse makes on the ground. Every run is another step closer.

We seem to lose our breath simultaneously because we both come to a screeching halt, our heads between our knees as we fight for more breath.

"I'm winded." I swear under my breath, aching for something wet down my throat. Evan chuckles, his cheeks dyed red from all the running. I don't even notice the ache in my leg anymore, I feel too exhilarated. There isn't even an ache.

"Don't keep doing that," Evan straightens up and pulls my hair behind my ears, "you'll be sick."

"Oh," I mumble. "Gross." His hands still stay tangled in my hair, even as I straighten my posture.

"Evan."

"Hmm?"

"What are you doing?"

"What?" He pulls his hand out of my hair and lets it drop to his side. "Sorry. Uh, got my hand stuck."

"Right," I say, and then realizing I have made it awkward, I grab the chicken cage and his hand, whispering one word into his ear.

"*Run.*"

And we do.

Chapter Thirteen

And we run until we can't anymore. Until we are suddenly trapped between two police cars. My heart is pounding in my chest, my ears are ringing, but I have never felt more alive in any moment, in any second than I do right now. There's something exhilarating about it all. Evan's equally as breathless, holding his hand to his chest as he wheezes.

"Holy shit." I pant. "Why are they after us?"

Evan looks up and grabs my arm, pulling me and the crate of chickens down an alleyway. The chickens are going insane, making more and more noise. I'm so confused at this point I don't even know what to say, or even why the police are following us. Evan paid for the chickens. He said he did. I don't understand what we have done wrong. *Why did Evan say to carry on running?* I don't know what his plan is now.

The police are here, and we can't exactly stay hidden. My chest squeezes with worry and I know I should be angry that he isn't giving me an answer, but I am too exhilarated and drummed up on adrenaline to make sense of my emotions right now. I lean against the wall and stare at the crate of chickens on the floor.

"Fuck," Evan finally swears under his breath. He eyes the crate between us and swears again. It suddenly hits me. He never paid.

"Evan." I reach for him and I don't have to stretch far; the alleyway is small.

"You paid, right?" I question, but I know the answer. He doesn't meet my eyes and any exhilaration I'd been feeling drains.

"Jesus Christ Evan!" I cry, leaning back against the wall of the alleyway and squeeze my eyes shut. I can feel him start to pace and he mutters something under his breath.

"Evan, why didn't you—"

"I'm sorry, Kayla, alright!" he snaps and I open my eyes. He glares at me, and I am a bit taken aback by it. It definitely shuts me up for the moment. The chickens are going crazy, making all sorts of noises, and I kneel beside them, trying to figure out what to do.

"I did this," Evan suddenly mumbles and then louder, "*I stole* the chickens. This is my fault. I left my money in my suitcase back at the hotel. I realized on the way up there and I tried to distract the man whilst you were gathering the chickens. I guess the man got the gist of what I was doing. It's so fucking stupid, and I was going to give them back to the man after we had used them for the prank," he explains, stressfully tearing a hand through his hair. "I will tell them it was all me, that it was my fault."

My eyes widen. "You aren't serious?"

Evan looks uncomfortable. "I know it was stupid,"

"*Stupid?* Evan, it was sheer fucking idiocy! We're about ten seconds away from getting arrested. I can't believe this. I can't believe I trusted you. I am so stupid. *I'm* the stupid one." I rub my temples and snap my head in the direction of voices. They're here, the police.

"I can't believe I am going to be arrested for stealing some chickens!" I almost laugh. "This is not how I pictured my first arrest would go."

"Oh yeah?" Evan raises a curious eyebrow, looking cheeky all of a sudden. It's not the time or the place to be joking around. "How exactly did you think you'd get arrested?"

I roll my eyes. "Well, it certainly wasn't for stealing six chickens. It might have been from really letting go, like doing a protest for equal rights or something," I propose, though as soon as I say it, I realize it sounds lame.

"Wow." Evan breathes. "That's *really* letting *go*."

A police officer approaches. He has found us first. I watch as he takes a wary step towards us, no gun or other weapons in sight. He eyes me over, and I realize I am probably the easier arrest. He confirms this and slips a pair of handcuffs out of his pocket and talks to me. I don't know what he is saying but he makes a turning movement with his index finger and I spin around and let him cuff me.

I'm so going to hell for this.

I try my best to stop myself from crying, but the tears threaten to spill more than ever, and I feel like every shitty thing that has happened since I stepped into this country has somehow been made worse through one single person, and that's when I can feel my cheeks get wet.

Evan, also cuffed, shoots me a pained look. I know he is sorry. But I can't bring myself to care, not now. Not with this happening. The cop starts to read me my rights or what I believe to be it as we walk towards the car. I can feel them, the eyes of passersby, the gawks. I can feel every stare like it hits every molecule of my body and I cry harder.

"Kayla." Evan's voice is soft as we stand on either side of the car doors.

I shake my head, the tears still coming. "No, Evan,"

"Please, I'll make this better,"

I continue to shake my head. "I hate you." I climb into the backseat.

•   •   •

Evan's knees are curled up to his chin and the dingy holding cell smells of pee and tobacco. I'm desperate for the toilet, but the hole in the wall has a stained rim and shit stuck in the gaps. It makes me want to gag. The floor, although dirty, is better than the bench that is loosely screwed into the wall on the right-hand side. I haven't seen anyone other than Evan for over an hour and I'm sure I'm entitled to a phone call.

I have stopped crying. Mainly because as we were getting processed, my mug shot would have been horrendous—okay, more horrendous—and if I'm honest, I don't know if I have any more tears. I feel like I've spent the entire week in and out of tears. I'm not sure if it's normal to cry this much.

Evan's voice is croaky. "Are you going to talk to me?"

I know he's sorry, he has been telling me every two minutes since we have arrived, but I don't have anything to say to him right now. I turn away.

"Please, Kayla."

"Take a hint, Winters," I say as nastily as I can, but it just comes out pathetic.

"Fine." He stands up and begins to pace the cell. "You know what? This is *why*, this is why I can't be dealing with girl drama or trying to make an effort for somebody else because while I do, I am getting it thrown back in my face."

I make a face not understanding how this is relevant and turn around. "Are you kidding?"

"I'm over it."

And I stand. "You have got us both arrested, Evan. I mean is your ego so inflated that you can't understand that my chances to any major colleges are now gonna be destroyed?" I fold my arms and wait for a response, but he only blinks.

"And what about yours?" I continue. "This is going on my record. I will be asked at every interview I ever have about this incident and have to somehow explain how my neighbor made me think it was a good idea to steal some chickens when we were in Italy. Do you think anybody is ever gonna take me seriously ever again? I certainly wouldn't. You're so self-centered, all you ever think about is yourself and never how you could implicate other people. I hate you, okay. *I hate you* and I definitely don't want to talk to you."

"Wow." Evan laughs sarcastically. "I'm self-centered? All you have been doing this entire trip is whining about *yourself.* Not once have you expressed a thought about your best friend or anyone else. It's all about what Kayla wants. Oh, too bad Kayla's been cheated on, let's all fall over ourselves to cheer her up. Oh, Kayla has been injured. Let's bring havoc to the kitchen to make sure Kayla is alright. Oh, and what about back at home eh? When I needed you, you shoved me away so quick I pretty much toppled backward."

"What the hell are you talking about?" I'm yelling now, amazed.

"A year ago, around midnight when I knocked on your bedroom window and asked if I could borrow your restroom. What did you do? You told me to shove it. You slammed the window down so hard I nearly fell out that fucking tree. You didn't even bother to acknowledge why I might have needed your bathroom at that time of night," Evan shouts, but it's almost as if he can't be bothered like he's defeated. But I do remember. It was late summer, and the weather was warm, too hot to sleep even with their aircon on, so I had opened the window.

"What?" I didn't expect this. "I mean, why did you need it?"

Evan laughs again. "Well, it's a bit freaking late now, isn't it?"

"Evan."

"My Dad," he starts. "He went into another full-scale argument with my mom and pretty much ripped the toilet from the floor with a baseball bat over something stupid. It's beside the point. I needed you, and yet again, you proved that you can't care about anyone but yourself."

I can't breathe. "Evan." I part my lips to say something more, but I don't know what to say. I remember hearing it. It was what was keeping me up. The night comes back to me and I remember every moment.

It is my turn to apologize. "Evan, I didn't realize. I'm so sorry,"

He shuts his eyes. "I've only ever tried with you, Kayla. You're the one who instigated this mutual hatred between the two of us. I realized that night you were nothing but a spoiled little brat."

It hurts. And not because he is the one saying it, but because it is true. I had been the one to hurt him first, properly. I had been the bitch.

"Evan," I touch his arm, but he pulls away. *I'm so sorry*, I want to say. *I am so sorry I wasn't there for you.* But he's not ready to hear it—not yet. And I realize then too, maybe I'm not ready to say it either.

Chapter Fourteen

It's late, or at least I think it is from the fact that the holding cell is growing darker. The clock on the wall has been stuck on quarter past three since we arrived and unless time has stopped, it's wrong. There's only one small, dingy light that hangs crookedly from the ceiling and it doesn't illuminate much of anything. Evan's sulking, his back to me on the bench, and he has been muttering something to himself on and off for a while now. I'm sitting the farthest away I can get, my back pressed between the cold bars and my legs sprawled out in front of me. I can't stop thinking and there isn't much else to do in here besides think. My mind feels like it's trying to unscramble a million things at once, each one getting more tangled in the mess of more thoughts. I look over to Evan and I know I've got to say something. I have to make it right.

I sit up slowly and cross my legs. "Evan," I start.

"Hmm?" I don't catch it at first, convinced he's still ignoring me.

"I'm really sorry," I apologize, but it comes out as one long syllable, so I try and clarify. "I'm sorry for shutting you out, I'm sorry for what I said and most of all I'm sorry for making you feel the way I only ever thought you made me feel. I'm sorry for starting this...*thing* between us and I'm sorry it ended up this way. I don't hate you. I don't think I ever have. I'm just really sorry."

Evan remains silent, but his back begins to turn, and I squint in the dim light to make out enough of his face. His eyes are red and his lips a similar shade as if he's been chewing on them for the last couple of hours. "I'm not stupid you know."

I sigh. "Evan, I know what I said, but I didn't mean it."

He lies on his back and crosses both arms behind his head. "I knew about Jess. I knew that she had pretty much every guy wrapped around her finger, and I couldn't blame her. Obviously, at first it bothered me, and I tried everything to stop feeling anything for her. Ignoring her didn't work, being a dick didn't work either and eventually, there is only so much you can do before you just give up. I kinda reckoned that *any* form of relationship with her was better than not having her in my life at all." I furrow my eyebrows, surprised the conversation has led back here, but it's clearly on his mind.

He sits up, his hair matted and falling messily over his forehead. It almost covers his green eyes, but they stare at me through the dim lighting. "What I'm getting at is that I knew Jess always called herself *free-spirited* or whatever and she didn't do commitments. She hated the thought of relationships or being tied down to pretty much anything. She thought the whole thing of being with one person for the rest of her life was boring and ordinary and I guess I liked that edge about her." He swallows a laugh. "The point is I knew about this the entire time and I still couldn't help the way I felt about her."

I chew the outside of my lip. Seeing Evan Winters like this—emotional—makes me feel funny, on the edge like I'm waiting for the punch line of a really shit joke. "Evan, you don't have to talk about this if you don't want to," I say because I don't know how else to stop the feeling inside my stomach, but I can't help but want to know what made her so fascinating. How Jess, of all people, managed to make loner and bad boy

Evan Winters' cold heart beat. And I realize that this isn't even about him because I'm desperate to feel the same. I want someone to look at me the way Evan Winters looks at a girl who is half of the person he is. I want someone to be completely mesmerized, to talk about me like I'm the single and most important person on earth.

Evan sighs. "That first night at the airport, once we had landed, I watched Ben wrap his arm around you and smile into your hair and make you smile despite the situation. Don't take this the wrong way, but I don't think I would have noticed if he was looking at you as he was doing this, but he wasn't. He was looking at Jess, and she was grinning at him like he knew her biggest secrets and I realized then how much I had been ignorant to the looks he had been giving her over the last couple of weeks before we flew out here. The visits behind the sheds to have a smoke when I had never seen Ben Moore smoke a cigarette in his life. The hushed conversations besides his car before you arrived at school." He stops talking and looks at me and my stomach flips, the sick feeling returning, and I want to scream at the idiot I've been.

"So anyway, I followed the two of them that night and I saw them, and the sickest part is that Ben saw me looking and he *smiled.*"

My mouth opens. "Oh my God."

"And as if by magic you turn up, loud and unaware and it was just *so* perfect. I was so angry, and I took it out on you. You were so blind, and I knew I owed nothing to you, but I couldn't find the words to tell you, so I showed you." He rubs the back of his neck with one hand and bends his fingers back to stretch them. "I knew I was being a dick, but I couldn't bring myself to care about your feelings after—"

"After what I had done to you." I look down at my feet.

He continues, "But I watched your face, and it was like watching myself suddenly go from floating to drowning in just a second. I had let myself revel in your pain for a split-second, but I felt for you, God I promised myself that I would help you get your own back on that dickhead, if not for you then for me."

I let out a sharp breath and stand. Evan stands too and walks towards the bars and leans against them. "Loving someone is bullshit. It makes you the best and the worst person you can ever be, and it reminds you constantly why you need to be a better version of yourself just to be worthy of that person. And Jess is impossible *not* to love. She's the light at the end of a firecracker and the chorus of every song," he describes her with a small smile on his face.

"She's a spitfire," I say. "Utterly flammable and dangerous but nearly impossible to take your eyes off."

Evan looks at me properly for the first time since we argued, for longer than a second. He looks exhausted, rugged and he needs a shower, but he also looks defeated and alone and I have never wanted to comfort someone more in any moment than now.

"A spitfire," he says slowly, agreeing. I meet his eyes. "Exactly."

"I won't begin to suggest that I know what you're feeling," I say. "But I know what it feels like to love someone who doesn't love you back." He doesn't say anything because he doesn't have to. Some things are just really that simple.

Living isn't about how long you're alive; it's about what you do in your life. You can live a thousand lives and still be unhappy. Knowing what it means to be alive is the only feeling worth all the pain and the baggage it brings. If Evan Winters has taught me anything, it's to live a little.

The sudden sound of keys rattling makes me snap out of my thoughts and I spin around in time to see the cop who arrested us slotting the keys into the lock. He looks at the two of us, raises an eyebrow and then points to the phone on the side of the wall.

"Telephone," is all he says and leaves the door open. I am the first to move and pick up the phone, punching in a number.

"Ciao, Mariana Hotel Plaza."

I hold my breath, relieved I have got the number right and close my eyes, my body resting on the side of the phone box. "Hello, could you dial me through to room 205? Tell him Kayla Burns is calling for Adam."

Chapter Fifteen

I wish I could be one of those people who doesn't ever need anyone or anything to get by in life. I wish I could be one of these people who could stop feeling so strongly about things, but most of all, I wish I could make the right choices. I wish, and I wish and at the end of the day I could wish for anything or everything and it will never come true because wishing never achieves anything. It's only wishful thinking, which is why sitting here listening to Evan make his one phone call is wishful thinking, because I am hoping he doesn't call her, *Jess*.

But he does, and a part of me realizes that of course, he would call her, he doesn't have anyone else. Logically, Jess has been the most consistent person in his life that is here in Italy, and logically it makes sense he would ring her out of all people because she is the only person he can turn to. Logically everything makes sense, but I wish it wouldn't and I'm back to the same cycle.

And I can deny it all I want but this wishful thinking is down to me. I can't help finding myself wanting to be the one Evan can count on. I'm not sure if it's because all of this time we have been spending together, or whether it's because I feel guilty for the first time, but the feeling doesn't suppress itself even as he ends his call and heads back to the holding cell where I have taken up residence on the bench he was on earlier.

He sits beside me without a word. I glance at him from the corner of my eye and figure that even through this shit storm of a couple of weeks, and even from being arrested, I still cannot predict what Evan Winters will do or who he is anymore. Or if I ever really knew. I feel as if I have drawn a picture of Evan Winters and I've got to rub the entire thing out and start again, the end result completely different. But that's the thing: there is no black and white picture of him. He's a grey area, swimming around in a pool of unpredictability. And it makes me nervous.

I place my head on his shoulder, mostly out of curiosity, but equally because I want some comfort and I'm surprised to feel his arm snake around my back and find my waist. He pulls me into him and rests his head on top of mine.

We sit there for a while, both meshed in our own individual thoughts, consumed by the place we are in. Silence devours the air, but it's welcome. My thoughts are a blur, but I know one thing: I need Evan at this moment, and he needs me too. And it isn't wishful thinking.

•   •   •

It turns out someone does speak English here. At around seven that night, a bald man reaching a total height of five foot three steps into the holding cell both Evan and I have been confined in for nearly fourteen hours, briefcase in hand, and introduces himself as William Fisher. He's a lawyer and continues to tell us he only aims to please and it sounds like something out of a creepy porno. But he also tells us Adam sent him and that's got to mean something, so we listen. He definitely likes to talk and begins with why it has taken him three hours to get here. If you're interested, it had something to do with puke and a diaper and I don't want to gross you out anymore.

William gives one of the cops a look and they open the cell and he leads us towards a small room which he explains is where the police usually conduct interviews. He tells us it's a private place to talk and everything we say will be kept only between the three of us.

William tells Evan and me to take a seat, and we sit side by side each other. I can't help but think how we look like an episode of *Law and Order.* We are asked to reiterate what happened and Evan does most of the talking as William writes it down. I add in a few points here and there, but mostly listen to what Evan says and how he makes every effort to seem as though it is entirely his fault. It makes me uncomfortable; there are two of us here after all.

Evan—who had been collective and calm since speaking to Jess on the phone—finishes explaining in full detail why we ended up running around Rome with a cage of half a dozen chickens. William places his pen down, leans back in his chair and then laughs a loud, giggly, but choked laugh that you'd expect from a four-year-old girl, not a middle-aged man.

It takes me by surprise. Evan too.

"You can't be serious," William says between laughs. He has been pretty professional until now and I'm beginning to think Adam picked the last lawyer he could find. "I'm defending two mindless teenagers who thought that stealing some chickens from an angry Italian farmer was a smart idea?" It's a rhetorical question and even if it isn't, neither Evan nor I dignify him with an answer.

William looks over to me and ceases his laughter. "You're awfully quiet," he comments, smoothing his tie and readjusting himself on the chair.

"Well, there isn't much more to be said other than knowing what you're gonna do to help us out of this," I reply grumpily. "And laughing at us is just wasting our time."

William raises an eyebrow at Evan. "She's a bit fiery, isn't she? I bet you struggle to keep her on a leash, but yes, Miss Burns, I have a solution."

"Awesome," Evan jumps in, dismissing his comment. "We're all ears."

William looks pleased with himself and claps his hands together. "It's a bit comprehensive really, and it will take a lot of apologies and maybe some money here and there—"

"How much money?" I interrupt.

"Not now, Kayla." Evan chides me. He is tense.

"But before you know it, you'll be back in the free world with gelato and lots of kissing you haven't been able to do in here," William finishes with a wink at the two of us.

"Oh," I say, and then a moment passes, and I twig. "*Oh, no.* Me and him." I point between Evan and me. "Nada. *No.*"

"Whatever you say."

"William," I start.

"Kayla." He doesn't look up from his paperwork.

"Look, how can we be more helpful?" I ask, shifting in the plastic chair. It is one of those old ones that squeaks every time you move, making you believe that one wrong move could leave you airborne with your legs sticking up at unattractive angles.

"Do exactly what you're doing," William tells us. "Don't speak to anyone other than yourselves, try your best not to steal any more chickens and hope to God that I can talk to this farmer fella and sort this out for you both."

And just like that, I find myself signing away a contract to an Italian pensioner promising to not only profusely apologize, but to return all the chickens to him along with a small lump of cash for the trouble we caused.

It is better than jail, I tell myself bitterly.

When Evan and I are escorted by a police officer to the front desk, he turns to me and chuckles. "I'm going to have to think of another revenge plot."

I think about punching him or screaming at him that now really isn't the time, but instead, I grin. "I guess you better get plotting then."

•   •   •

We are released on the conditions that we a) apologize to Mr. Emmanuel in person and in writing, b) we return the chickens unharmed as soon as we got out, and lastly, write him a cheque of what figured (roughly) to be a hundred dollars in American money for loss of business of those six chickens and the trouble we have caused him. William thinks we've won the lottery with this deal, especially being foreigners.

The cop behind the desk slams something down on the counter. *"Una gomma da masticare, un portafoglio e un mazzo di chiavi."* He has got Evan's pack of gum, his wallet and a set of keys on the desk. I didn't have anything with me.

"You ready?" Evan turns to me.

"I'm ready for freedom." I rub my shoulders.

"Aspettare!"

We spin around, and the officer is holding up the cage of chickens. "Fuck sake," Evan mutters under his breath and walks back to take them out of his hand. An officer is waiting for us the other side of the door to take us to the farmer's house and as we are buzzed through and step outside, I turn to Evan and laugh.

"Freedom's good."

Evan laughs back. "Babe, freedom's fucking fantastic."

Chapter Sixteen

Freedom feels like the first time you realize that monsters don't exist. Or in this case, the fantasy kind. You only learn later that the real monsters look like you and me. But freedom feels like relief. And relief feels fucking amazing.

The chickens complain with another squeaky clucking sound as the police car rattles over another bump as we make the painful journey towards Mr. Emmanuel's house. He lives on top of a long hill with a path to the house equally as long. The sky is dark, but for several days now there hasn't been any heavy rain. The wind is still stronger than I would like. Walking in the wind is like trying to push your way through a pull door. It's pretty much impossible. But it's nothing like it has been, and I am so thankful.

Evan's quiet the entire journey, his cell phone spinning in one of his hands. He drums his fingers on the seat in front of him and keeps his eyes locked out of the window. I am desperate to say something to take his mind off thinking about her, but I don't know the right thing to say. I contemplate my conversations with Evan over the last fourteen hours and consider if anything I really said to him has sunk in. I think about the fact that my opinion probably—if not definitely—holds little weight over Evan Winter's actions and I won't lie and say it doesn't bother me.

These last fourteen hours something has happened, something has changed.

Call it guilt, but whatever it is, it's eating away at me. These last hours have changed something between us. I'm starting to forget the reasons why I disliked him for so long, and why I was the way I was to him. For years it seems like it was integrated inside of me to be standoffish and rude to a boy that, in theory, really hasn't done anything wrong to me. I was the one who started it all. Sure, the boy has his flaws, and I can recount many occasions where being his next-door neighbor has left me cringing, but he's also not half the things I always thought he was.

And despite it all, the boy is still here, he's always been *there*. He made the plan back at the airport; he's the one who kept us from starving to death. He's the one who carried me away from the window when it shattered and injured my leg. He's the one who showed me the truth, no matter how painful. This isn't what you do when you don't like someone. This isn't what a bad person does.

Everything has changed because now I look at the boy to my right and I know he's my friend.

Once we reach the top of the hill, the cop pulls to a shaky stop and I snap out of my train of thought and unbuckle my seatbelt. Evan leans down and picks up the chicken cage beside his feet and glances at me once as if he's trying to communicate something with his eyes, but I don't get what he's trying to say. I do my best to force a smile. We have to get this over and done with.

The police officer opens the door for me and I climb out. I try to say thank you in Italian which is the only word I know, but he just blinks at me as if I'm speaking gibberish and watches as Evan meets us the other side of the car. He bumps into my side like he isn't watching where he is going, but after the third or maybe the fourth time he does it, I notice him lingering close, the hairs of his arm grazing mine. I suck in a breath because I'm not used to this sudden comfort between us, friends or not. But I guess the saying really is true: jail does change you.

It all happens swiftly. We knock twice on the door and Mr. Emmanuel opens it, peers at the two of us with a daggered look, and staggers out, walking stick in hand. My chest tightens, and I feel worse than I do already. We stole from a man who can't walk, and I wish it didn't, but it makes the whole thing a lot worse. I think about Mom and how disappointed she would be with me right now and dread the moment I arrive home and face the music. I'm still seventeen, so no doubt she will have been informed or will be as soon as possible.

The cop is behind us, I can feel his stare burning to my back as we do the exchange. When the cop starts to speak to the farmer, we hand him over an envelope of money. The farmer looks at the two of us expectantly and holds one of his hands out for the chicken cage. I make the first move since Evan stands quietly beside me and hand him the cage.

I cough, clearing my throat. "Sir, I speak for both Evan Winters and me here when I say that we are both incredibly sorry for taking your chickens without your consent. We did not mean to cause you any distress and therefore present you with this money for any business lost in the process. We have returned the chickens to you unharmed and hope you take this as a sign that we did not want to cause you any more heartache. Once again, we apologize," I speak so formally I'm almost winded by my own performance.

I can feel Evan relax beside me, his shoulders slumping. He's pleased I delivered well too, despite already deciding that he was going to be the one that was going to do the talking earlier. Don't ever trust a boy.

The farmer just blinks and looks to the police officer for help, who begins translating everything I have just said. Once the police officer has finished, the farmer nods, accepting the envelope and cage and places them beside him. He nods once more and then smiles, throwing his arms around the two of us and his walking stick drops to the ground and clatters. I freeze, alarmed by the sudden forgiveness and snuffle a laugh into the farmer's chest.

Mr. Emmanuel lets us go and presses his palms together, his hands shaking. I lean down and pick up his walking stick and hand it to him.

He looks like he is going to well up in tears. *"Buisness è stata molto lenta. Questo mi aiuterá."*

Evan looks to the police officer for translation advice and he tells us that he has said that his business is very slow, and this is going to help him. It's a thank you I didn't expect to get.

"You're welcome," Evan speaks for the first time and shakes the man's hand.

The farmer smiles and turns around to shut his door. We stare at the closed door for a moment, the peeled paint and the smell of bread putting me on edge like I'm expecting him to open the door again with a gun or something.

Evan touches my arm. "Time to go."

I look down at his fingers that loosely hang over my elbow and I think Evan catches me staring because he drops his hand and adds, "That went very well. I thought we were being pranked or something."

"Tell me about it," I agree.

"But we still have a problem," Evan continues as we start our descent down the path.

"Which is?"

"We have a brilliant revenge plan but now we don't have any chickens."

I think about my response before replying. It takes me the whole way to the car to realize what the plan is and how we will execute it.

"Leave it to me, Winters," I finally say. "I have it covered."

•   •   •

Two steps forward, my breath heavy from running up three flights of stairs, I reach Evan's door. His room has moved since our arrest, something about overcrowding. I think the fifth floor has the larger rooms which I personally don't think is fair for Evan to have by himself, and after being released from jail. But this boy's luck is endless.

Once we had arrived back at the hotel, Evan and I both stood shocked, barely in the double doors, as our classmates filled the hotel lobby, *clapping* as we came in. Yes, clapping as if we'd won the Noble Peace Prize or something. Mrs. Scott was the first to greet us with a hug and patted our backs, telling us she was incredibly pissed (being the operative word) that we both managed to get arrested on her watch, but both happy that we handled it responsibly and didn't end up in jail. She never mentions whether she has informed our parents.

Our friends were there too, of course. Sophie had hugged me the moment she laid eyes on me, eager for a blow by blow account of the whole experience. Damon and Tom had simply smirked as Evan explained some of the stories to them, immersed about what had happened but acting like this was a normal Thursday for him. I had spotted Ben out of the corner of my eye as Sophie led me through the crowd of people to somewhere quieter, but in truth, I had been on the lookout for Adam, eager to thank him and hit him for getting us the weirdest but most reasonable lawyer in all of Rome. But instead, my eyes had landed on Ben, who stood alone by the reception desk. He had mouthed something like *'I'm sorry'* which I let hang in the air like dead fish on a clothesline.

It's been hours since then and I knock twice on Evan's door once more, convinced he doesn't hear it. I think rationally to myself. Maybe he's in the shower and this is an inconvenience, not to mention awkward if he's answering the door in just his towel. How can I propose what I'm about to without this sounding incredibly suggestive? Or maybe he thinks it's room service and that I will use my own key to open the door. But room service doesn't exist here, not with what's going on. Whatever situation I come up with, it leaves me standing the other side of this door, and then walking away.

Get a grip. I spin back around and urge myself to knock again. This time I can hear Evan's heavy footsteps reach the door as my knuckle rattles twice. He swings the door open, the door caught on the carpet.

Evan frowns. The room is dark, and the hallway light illuminates his face. He looks exhausted like he's just woken up.

"Kayla?" he poses it as a question but it's obviously me. I notice his voice is husky and he's not wearing a towel which makes what I am about to propose a lot less awkward. "Come in," he says when I don't say anything.

I do, closing the door behind us and fiddle to find the light switch. Now that I'm here, I don't know what to say or how to propose this without it sounding weird. I shove my hands into my sweater and fiddle with my fingers, antsy.

"Um, Evan, I…"

"I know what you're going to say," he says before I get a chance to say anything else.

I look at him, surprised. "You do?"

"I think I've known for a long time." He smiles and sinks into the couch beside him. "You're utterly in love with me and my charming looks and it has just taken you this breathtaking moment as you ran three flights of stairs without obviously using the elevator, like *normal people,* to realize this." He smirks at me playfully.

I smack his arm and sit beside him. "Don't be big-headed," I warn. "I'm surprised your ego can fit in this room to begin with."

"It fits comfortably, thank you for asking." He winks.

"Oh, and I can promise you one thing, I will definitely not fall in love with you."

Evans grins. "That's music to my ears, Kayla."

I shake my head. I came here for a reason and not for some mediocre banter. "Right."

"Well, come on," he prompts. "What is it that you've been dying to tell me?"

"I have figured it out," I tell him. "Now, I know it's a bit out of the blue and weird but I heard Jess's friends speaking in the hallway about how 'close' we had gotten recently. This made me think of the one and only piece of revenge that happens to benefit us both with hopefully long-lasting results."

Evan's eyebrows raise, his expression letting me know he's interested. I'm cautious to tell him, worried he'll laugh or something, but even more worried he won't go along with it.

"Be my fake boyfriend, Evan Winters," I propose. "I promise never to love you, care for you or well, you get the idea." I pause and look up for his reaction, as I have been saying this to my lap. "What do you say?" my voice trembles slightly.

Evan sits up, his face suddenly breaking into a grin. "The day I'm proposed to has *finally* arrived. I mean, don't get me wrong, I thought I'd be doing the grand speech or whatever. By the way, yours need working on."

I lean over and smack his chest, but my hand lingers. "You bastard."

Evan looks down at my hand and pulls me to him. When I'm close enough, he ruffles my hair. "Now, now, you can't be calling your boyfriend every name under the sun, now can you?"

Chapter Seventeen

Evan's first suggestion is for me to stay the night. I know, my thoughts exactly. You have got to be kidding. I refuse to sleep with Evan to keep the ruse up, or even camp in his bedroom for the night if *this* is the state he gets his room in over a couple of days. I kick an open chicken box from the floor by accident as I stand up, a cold piece of chicken flying across the floor. Since the arrest, Evan has gone into survival mode, stuffing his face with everything that he can possibly make room for without puking.

"Oh, for God's sake." He narrows his eyes as he makes a face. "I didn't mean it like that."

"Then don't say, 'hey, why don't we sleep together tonight?' and then you tell me that you wouldn't think someone didn't mean it like *that*," I retort back, frustrated.

"You seriously think anything frisky is gonna happen behind these doors?" Evan questions, shaking his head. He picks the remote control up, despite the storm only allowing the cable television to give us three channels out of the hundreds. "The only thing that's gonna happen behind here will be *you* ordering room service for *me* while I shower."

"There isn't any room service you idiot, we have just been a part of a disaster. I don't see any butlers running around here, do you?"

Evan rolls his eyes. "I need a shower."

"Oh, a shower." I raise an eyebrow. "So, you know what that is?" It's a crappy comeback but it's all I got. I try to make it obvious and stare at the state of his room to suggest that's what I mean.

"Hey." He grins slightly, arching his back against the couch as he reaches for an itch. "What did I say about being a shit to your boyfriend?"

"It works two ways you know." I fold my arms. "You have to be a *lovely* boyfriend to me if you want me to lick your fucking feet in return."

He laughs. "Alright then, fair enough."

"So..." I flop down on the armchair beside the window. The outdoors takes my attention away from what I'm about to say for a moment. Since the storm, the sun breaking out from behind the thick layer of clouds has made the air warmer. Grey covers the world as far as I can see, the ruins becoming more apparent every day. After arriving back at the hotel, Sophie had told me that a volunteer clean-up team at the hotel had been created to help the local area clear as much glass, rubble and anything removable before the professionals managed to get to the rest of it. She told me she had put my name down, and it makes me good to know I can give back even in a small way.

"Earth to Kayla?"

"Uh *blug* at?" I say, completely unintelligible.

Evan frowns. "What's wrong with you? You speak all high and mighty and then go off into space the next minute. Don't tell me you're schizophrenic. I can't deal with that."

I stare. "You know your inability to recognize serious illness is utterly appalling. Go read a book or something."

He chuckles, standing so that he can put the crap that he has accumulated on the floor into the trash and ruffles my hair, again. "So?"

"So, what?"

"I don't know, you're the one who said it."

"Oh, right," I pause. "So how is this going to work? I mean, we're going to need some sort of story of how we got together, blah blah blah."

"I have the perfect thing in mind," Evan replies swiftly, barely even thinking about it at all.

"Oh yeah, what's that? Let me guess, Kayla falls in love with sexy god Evan Winters in their dangerous escapade to steal some chickens. She announced her feelings in the holding cell and a massive make-out session commenced alongside a little feel of the boob." I smirk at Evan. "Sound about right?"

"You said it, not me."

"We all know what you were thinking."

He cocks an eyebrow. "There is no 'we'. There is only us."

"Don't be smart, Evan." I rock my foot against the carpet, an agitated move my mom always does when she can't be bothered with the conversation.

"Then don't be dumb, Kayla."

I rub my hands against my jeans and think about a logical reason why, over two weeks ago, two hateful strangers would suddenly start dating. "We should just say this: that we realized that somehow or somewhere along the way we really do like each other. That you can't choose who you fall in love with because if you did, you'd choose the wrong person."

Evan says nothing for a long moment. The pause seems to drag out and I'm convinced he isn't going to say anything because his lips barely move. And then all of a sudden, he throws his head back and lets out an almighty laugh. "Wow! That was beautiful."

"Piss off." My cheeks are warm though and I look at the clock.

Evan looks too. "We better get the show on the road then." He stands up and holds out his hand. "Coming, babe?"

• • •

THE WALK towards the dining room seems long and dragged out. Evan lets go of my hand as soon as we enter the elevator and I realize it's because nobody is there to look at us. As soon as the door chimes and they open, I grab Evan's hand again, which is sweaty and not exactly what I would call nice hand-holding, but it's comforting to know he feels as nervous as I do, so I don't bring him up on it.

"Maybe this is a bad idea," I mumble to him as we make our way past reception. The woman at reception gives me a confused expression; after all, she has witnessed the two of us arguing inexplicably since we arrived. I'm kind of glad she doesn't make a move to say anything though.

Evan sighs beside me. "Maybe it is, but Ben also needs someone to unlodge that stick up his ass. He's a dick Kayla, and he makes you feel like crap, so think about that while you're holding my sweaty hand and you're pretending to like me." He doesn't look my way once as he speaks but gives my hand a reassuring squeeze.

A strange feeling in the pit of my stomach stirs and I try to shrug it away.

You know in all those movies that have that hot guy and girl come around the corner and make this grand entrance into the cafeteria? Well, our entrance was a little like that; less of the hot and more of the gaping faces as we enter the room that currently is catering to far too many people.

I try not to throw up from the sudden attention, but I can feel myself getting judged by hundreds of eyes as if I'm standing here with my boobs out. I spot Sophie's dark hair near the front of the pack of people, her eyes wide and pupils dilated. She looks surprised and I don't hold my gaze on her for too long because it isn't her I want to see. Evan and I had let our friends onto our plan earlier to avoid this.

"Um," I break the tension and look at Evan, "our group is over there."

"Sure," Evan says through pressed lips. "Let's be going then." He lets go of my hand, aware of how sweaty it is now and presses a hand against the small of my back instead. This feels much nicer; his hands are warm despite the sweat I can't feel anymore and it tickles to be touched there. When we reach our table, Tom peaks at the two of us over a pair of glasses I've never seen him wear, his face completely whacked out and I realize Evan must not have told them yet. I sit, and Evan pulls the chair in for me. I thank him and wait for him to sit down. It feels too weird.

Tom coughs and raises an eyebrow as he stabs his pasta. "So, either I've been stuck in my room as the zombie apocalypse has happened or you two just came in here holding hands."

"I saw it too," Damon butts in, looking intently at the two of us. I notice how Sophie doesn't say anything, so when I look towards her, she looks hurt. She thinks I haven't told her and I remember she never replied to my text I sent her. She probably never saw it.

"It's not the zombie apocalypse or an asteroid or whatever you might say. It's a mutual decision that won't mean Evan will drag me back to jail," I start, turning to Evan, who steals a fry from Tom's plate. Evan throws his arm around my shoulders and moves closer to the table, ready to whisper to our friends.

"Meet my pretend girlfriend baby."

Chapter Eighteen

So, the day went a little like this: Evan had taken it upon himself to make sure that it was subtly obvious that we were 'dating'. He would press his hand against my back, not quite reaching round to hold me close to him but enough for it to look possessive and sort of romantic. He had also spoken only to me and our group—to which, the five of us have seemed to have remained mingled together since the storm. I think Evan's logic was that by shutting everyone out—a usual trick of his—it held many questions in the air, emphasizing the mysterious aura he is obsessed with having. *Were Evan and Kayla dating? What happened to Kayla and Ben? Is Jess going to be Evan's side girl?* I even heard one girl mutter that I was his side chick because (I quote) Jess's sex was *boring*. I wasn't sure whether or not to be flattered that this girl thought 'my sex' would be anything more interesting than Jess's would be. But I'm pretty sure the girl was only jealous because her ex-boyfriend slept with Jess six months or so back.

It was later that day at dinner, hundreds of us stacked around small tables, that I remember Adam. The dining room looked as if it could have been pretty nice in its element. The wallpaper is burgundy but is now peeling and a string of mold has started to gather around the rim of the ceiling. The light shade in the middle of the room is made of a nice-looking glass and is very big, but now drops to an angle. The tables that comfortably fitted five now uncomfortably fit ten, however, the majority of us ate with our plates on our laps. It has become more obvious whose table was whose. Families with young children got priority, then children that had been left alone, their parents dead or alive. Next the elderly and the disabled, but they came in shorter numbers. It was mostly our class who sat in the awkward areas.

I hadn't seen Adam for days now. *Days.* I had even gone to the trouble of asking Sophie, who was completely suspicious about me asking, if she knew. But she wasn't much help; she hadn't seen him for a while either. Damon overhears me asking and tells me the last he saw of Adam was when he was trying to help someone out of the elevator that had gotten stuck. The power has stopped working in some parts of the hotel, the increase for everything now so much higher but the generators simply can't handle it. The ones that aren't damaged are working at snail pace. More people are filing through each day and our rooms are now housing a couple more people each night. When the elevators do work, it takes a thousand years to get from one level to another, so most of us don't bother and just use the stairs.

I was beginning to worry, until I see him today, wandering through the dining room with his paper plate. It's stacked quite light and he seems to be in deep thought because his eyes wander past mine until he realizes who I am, and he looks back. I wave him over, indicating to the spare seat beside me and pull it out from the edge of the room for him. He gazes at it for what seems like forever, as if he's having an internal debate about whether or not he should sit there. I drop my eyes to my food plate and push it around aimlessly.

The next time I look up, Adam's gone.

• • •

I see Adam again that night, and this time I'm determined to talk to him. He's sitting alone by the pool, which of course is out of use and has gathered more debris and other bits and bobs from the fall out of the storm. It's late, almost three in the morning and the lights from outside my window have kept me awake. Since the shortage of space is growing more and more, I had told Sophie that I would be staying with Evan, making another bed spare in our room. She had agreed, knowing that it was for the good of someone else who had suffered terribly from the storm and, to be honest, it meant it looked better for our plan, so I didn't really care.

Evan had been surprised to know I was essentially moving in for however long but lapped up at the idea it would drive Ben nuts. We negotiated space, shower times in order to try and conserve hot water and even agreed on sleeping arrangements. We'd alternate nights on who got the bed and who got the couch. It was my turn on the couch tonight.

But I can't sleep. I must have been lying here for hours before I decide to go for a walk to help make me sleep. Tiptoeing around the room, I fumble to find some shoes and leave Evan sleeping as I make my way down the stairs and towards the pool. It's a cool night and I wrap my sweater around my arms, pulling at the ends to cover my fingers as I see Adam's shadowy figure sitting at the edge of the pool, looking at nothing in particular.

"I don't need a stalker right now," Adam declares as I sit down on the deck chair near him. I'm startled by the tone of his voice and frown in the dark. It's lit up enough that I can see his movements, but his back is to me and I can't make out what his face is telling me right now.

"Adam," I say. "It's not what you think." I move to sit on the edge of the pool beside him, the hairs on the back of my legs chilly as I stand up. The moon is peeking through a pool of clouds, trying to force its way through, but it can't quite manage it. I think of myself and how I wish I could just hide away forever. I want to be the moon.

Adam scoffs and snaps me out of it. "What on earth do you know about what I'm thinking?" He scoffs again, this time adding a shrug. "It's not like you've bore that in mind whilst you've been lying to me." He shifts, like he is trying to move away from me. I notice his voice is strained, his accent tugging at all his vocal chords. It kind of feels like a slap in the face and I'm not sure what I can do to make it better besides tell the truth.

"Evan and I aren't dating," I start. "I mean, not like really. It's fake. An elaborate plan to get some revenge on Ben…my ex-boyfriend. We're doing it primarily so that Ben can feel how much it hurts," I explain it as best I can, but Adam still looks unconvinced.

"That's childish," Adam says. "And seems far-fetched."

"But true," it's all I can say.

"So, Evan just happens to get what out of this plan? What's in it for him? You've been running around Rome with him. You got yourself into a situation with him where you ended up in jail, Kayla, and now you're telling me that this dating rumor is fake and the two of you are getting your own back on your ex-boyfriend?" He finally looks at me. "Please tell me that I'm not the only one who thinks that sounds ludicrous."

I run a frustrated hand through my hair. "Yes, that's what I'm telling you. I'm telling you that Evan is doing this for his own reasons, ones that aren't mine to tell. I'm telling you that I have zero romantic feelings towards Evan Winters because for the last three years he has done nothing but make my life hell. He's not the obvious choice, but this is all the reason why it makes him the most shocking person to be with."

"He's a bad person, Kayla." Adam turns to look at me, finally. "He does everything for personal gain, nothing he does is to help anyone else and I want to make sure you don't do anything else stupid or get yourself locked up for good."

"Adam." I reach out and grab his hand, leaning off the deck chair and to my surprise he lets me hold it. "You don't have to worry about Evan, you don't have to worry about any of that because this plan was my idea and I know what I'm doing. Please listen to what I am telling you. I'm telling you that you are the one I am interested in. I want to try this with you. However, it might work."

Adam chooses not to reply. Instead, he cups my face with his right hand and kisses me slowly at first, then it builds up in intensity. It's soft and sweet and makes me feel giddy and happy, and as we pull away, he looks at me with such an intense look I think I might just melt.

"I want that Kayla," he murmurs. "I want that too." He smiles against my lips and wraps his hand around my shoulder and runs his finger over my exposed skin. "But I can't be with you when I know you've got to be with him. I can't be second best, and I'm sure you understand that. I've got to leave soon but if you find you're ever in London or you find yourself in the position where this means more than any silly revenge plot then I'll be waiting."

Adam stands up and pulls me up with him, his hand cupping my cheek again and I let myself nuzzle into it despite feeling rejected. I'm determined to remember it, remember this feeling, remember this moment.

Chapter Nineteen

I think too much, that's a given. Every single thought becomes another thought, and that thought grows to become another one and so forth. My thoughts become so tangled together, I'm not sure how I have space to fit in them all in. Trying not to overthink is like trying not to breathe, it's impossible. But I crave a clear head, a simple headspace.

I'm lying on the couch, smothered in blankets and extra pillows I've pried off Evan's bed. It's my turn to sleep on the couch and without the thousands of throw pillows, I don't think I would get remotely comfy. I have buried myself deep within them, a pillow or two covering my face and I've got a couple prodding my leg up. The pain has dulled to pretty much nonexistent. The antibiotics I was prescribed doing its magic, but the ache is still there every time I bend, and my leg feels heavier than ever.

I am immersed in my thoughts. My mind wandering back and forth to Adam, his touch, his lips. My heart drums a little bit faster as I think back. My body tingling from the memory. I haven't seen Adam again since last night and I know nothing more can happen, but for now, I am allowing myself the pleasure of getting to think back, to reminisce if only for a moment.

And it is only for a moment because a noise from behind me jolts the thoughts away.

"Hey." The sound of the double doors prying open behind me and Evan's voice lingering in the air makes me sit up, a pillow or two rolling off my face and onto my lap.

He steps out of the shadows, shirtless and sleepy. He's running his hand through his hair, the strands sticking up at odd angles.

"Oh," I say, my voice croaky. "Did I wake you?"

"From your late-night escapades? No, I was already awake." He laughs lightly, his own voice hoarse. "I don't know where you keep disappearing off to so late at night."

I had gone for another walk this evening. A part of me hoping I run back into Adam again, but he was nowhere to be found.

"About that," I start. Evan walks over to the opposite couch and plops himself down. "Adam and I kissed." I don't know why I feel obligated to tell him. Maybe it's because despite this relationship being based solely on revenge and nothing more, I still feel like I have done something wrong. But maybe it's because of something else too. Maybe it's because now I know we are friends, that I can tell him things like this.

"And?" He sits up only slightly, getting comfy, he doesn't show any type of emotion and I realize I'm desperate to read his reaction. I don't know what I am quite hoping to find on his face though.

"What?" I reply sharply, waiting for some kind of inappropriate joke or witty remark from his end.

He snorts and looks directly at me. "And why would you feel the need to tell me that? It's not like we're actually dating, Kayla. I don't give a shit who you're banging as long as the plan works." But his voice sounds unconvinced, strained and he spits my name like its sour in his mouth. I'm a little taken back.

"Alright." I roll my eyes. "Way to put it subtly."

"Subtly is for the prudes of the world," Evan counters. "I've never been much of a prude."

I raise an eyebrow. "So the lack of subtlety has been lapped up by the gigantic size of your—"

"—dick?"

"Ego. I was going to say *ego*, Evan." I shake my head.

"Yeah, sure." He snorts again, this time louder.

I notice now that his sweats are slung low over his hips, his Calvin Klein boxers are poking out of the top of his waistband. *He looks good,* and the moment I think it, I have to snap my eyes away. I shouldn't be looking anywhere *near* that area of his body. I break it down to our conversation and grab another pillow.

The room falls silent and I turn my face away from Evan, snuggling deeper into the pit of pillows and blankets, trying to hide the fact I had looked even though I'm pretty sure I didn't make it obvious. I don't know why I'm blushing, but my cheeks are stained red and I can feel just how hot they are by putting the back of my hand to them. I try to shake it away as I listen to Evan shifting on the couch, trying to get comfy. I'm trying desperately to stop the heated cheeks that I don't realize until it happens that Evan says the only thing that could be deemed utterly out of the blue *ever*. Especially for us.

"Kayla,"

"What?" I pull a pillow off my face again and sit up properly this time, so I'm facing him. The room is dark, so I pray my cheeks aren't visible.

"Do you want to watch a movie?"

And I laugh because it's four in the morning and I have been thinking just about anything else than watching a movie with Evan Winters. I laugh because his expression at me laughing is something out of a book, priceless and completely wacky. I laugh because Evan is trying *not* to laugh at how ridiculous my laugh has gotten.

I giggle uncontrollably, and soon Evan is sputtering too. I'm not too sure why it's so funny, but it just is. I chuck a long L-shaped pillow in Evan's direction and he tosses it back, smacking me right in the face. I don't attempt to say anything rude, despite the zip catching my lip and makes it sting. I just carry on laughing, pulling myself out of my pit and letting the blankets and pillows tumble around me. I grab two pillows, arming myself against Evan, and throw one underarm towards his chest and the other catching on the tip of his head.

"I see how it is." He narrows his eyes at me and then stands up on the couch.

And suddenly we're at war.

Both Evan and I are opposite each other, both equipped with several pillows, and we begin throwing them at each other. I duck as his largest pillow heads my way and skids against the blankets that I have been using on the couch. My balance fails despite avoiding the pillow, and I fall. I land with a thump, but it's a cushioned fall so it doesn't hurt too much.

"Giving up already are we?" Evan says playfully, taking this opportunity to toss another pillow my way that does hit me this time. "I didn't think you quit so easily."

"Who says I was quitting?" I stand up, pulling four extra small pillows under the nook of my arm. "I'm only just getting started."

"You asked for it, Kayla Burns." And before I realize what he's saying, he is stepping onto the coffee table between our two couches and makes the small step onto my couch. I let out a shriek as three pillows head in my direction and scramble to get the pillows I have been holding out from the nook of my arm. He lunges towards me and crashes down on the blankets in front, pulling my legs so that I fall with him. I let out a gasp, my breath catching, and my body exhilarated as we fall. He snorts out a chuckle; it's strangled with my elbow lying on his neck.

"Evan!"

Evan tumbles on top of me, his hair askew and his mouth parted. His leg hangs awkwardly off the couch and he inhales sharply.

"Fuck," he swears. "I didn't expect that to happen."

We both burst out into another fit of giggles and I raise my head to get some more air because he is still lying on me and trapping my flow of air. His face is so close that I notice things I haven't before like the freckles under his eyes and the way his nose is perfectly aligned on his face. I notice his cheekbones and the way his dimples show every time he laughs, and most of all, I notice how much I allow myself to notice all these little things.

I'm driving myself mad.

"You know," a voice mumbles from the shadows. My entire body freezes, tension lapping up the only air around me. I feel like, for a minute, I can't breathe as the voice continues. "If I hadn't seen Kayla earlier with that British guy, I'd have actually believed you two were together."

I look to my right as Evan's body becomes rigid and I see Jess with her arms folded, standing in the corner of the room. From where I'm lying, she's got a look on her face like she knows all of the secrets in the world.

I watch her unfold her arms and run her hand against the wall, tapping her nails as she does. "But then again, you two have hated each other since, like, forever. So, either you two have a *very* open relationship, or you are not actually dating." She steps forward.

I see her wearing a shirt that I know is Ben's because I've worn it once too. It makes me feel sick and I think if Evan doesn't get off me soon, I might just puke on him. I divert my eyes away from her and push Evan off me, aware that it probably won't do much to get us out of this one. The entire thing is ruined if Jess goes running back to Ben with what she knows. This entire thing would have been a complete waste of time.

Evan rubs the side of his head and actually starts to laugh. We both stare at him. This isn't really the time to be cracking a joke. "As if you'd know anything about morals when it comes to dating." His voice turns nasty. "You've been hooking up with another girl's boyfriend for months. You wouldn't know a moral relationship if it slapped you in the face."

Jess's mouth hangs open, her grin now dissolved into nothing. "Evan, you don't understand anything."

"And the funny thing is I thought I was in love with you. I thought I loved a girl who was passionate and funny, who cared about me and understood where I was coming from. But it's taken me this fucked up school trip and some dodgy weather to realize that I don't give a rat's ass about what you think anymore. I can't love someone who will blindly hurt someone else for their own pleasure. It's pretty sick if you ask me." Evan sounds so defiant, so strong that I can't help but feel proud of him. Here is the boy that can make a change. Here is the boy underneath the façade.

H steands up. "You don't know what is going on with Kayla and me. You certainly don't have a right to pry into our business. So, do us all a favor here and fuck the hell off."

So maybe I have got it all wrong.

Maybe Evan isn't this idiot who for years never spoke unless it was a snide dig at everyone and anyone. Maybe Evan isn't this ridiculously annoying boy next door who spent years raining hell on me over something I started in the first place. Maybe Evan is just a boy. Maybe I have known this all along. Maybe now I realize that Evan is the only person that, when it came down to it, had spent his time helping me get my own back on a guy who isn't even worth my breath. Maybe Evan is now one of my best friends, the sort of friend who you wished you always had.

The sort of friend who was always next door.

Chapter Twenty

Sophie has signed me up for cleanup duty. While I was fighting for my freedom in a jail cell, she had put my name down on the city board along with Evan, Damon, and Tom's to help clean up the streets. I'm not exactly sure what this is going to entail, after all, we are a bunch of seventeen- and eighteen-year-old kids. I'm not even sure what cleaning up the streets even means, or how literal it might be. But as we walk up to the location to where we are meeting our cleanup manager (a hairy guy with a monumental belly and a lazy eye), I realize we aren't exactly going to be litter picking.

There's something horrific about seeing a disaster right in front of your eyes. It always looks awful on TV, but when you're in the confines of your living room and it doesn't seem just so horrific. You'd pass a thought for all of the victims, thoughts to all the children who had parents searching for them or contribute to the money box at school or at your local church. Standing in front of it, however, is another story. A sight of rubble, broken lampposts and demolished buildings, my stomach lurches and my heart sinks so far that I feel as if I'm standing on it.

"I can't believe it," Tom mutters. He's quiet, but I pick up on it as he stands next to me. I shoot him a look out of the corner of my eye. He looks sick, the sort of look that resembles how I'm feeling. His glasses are perched just under the crook of his nose and he automatically adjusts them with his index and middle finger. "I know we were there, but the airport was only a fraction of the devastation. I haven't seen it this bad anywhere,"

My hands clutch around my jacket, the familiarity of it comforting me and I think about home. It's been nearly three and a half weeks since we first flew out here and I'm not sure how much longer I can stand being here. I'm desperate to see Mom, to see my little brother and to go home and put this all behind me. I know it's selfish to think I can put this away like a box under my bed. I know it, but I can't help thinking it.

"It's awful," I agree with Tom. I think about all the people who have ridden their bike down this street every day. I think about the girls who got kissed under the tree near the edge of the street. I think about the postman and the milkman and all those other jobs you really don't spare much time to think about. I think about the lives that have been crumpled because the weather decided that it wanted to wreak havoc. I think about everything we take for granted so easily at home. There's nothing left here.

The cleanup manager explains what we will be doing and rattles off a practiced speech about the city of Rome being incredibly grateful for our service. He sounds as bored as the stones look on this street full of chaos. He talks about damage to outside cities, to transport, and tells us that there is an end, but first, we have a duty to help, to rebuild.

My gaze momentarily flutters to Evan, who stands with crossed arms next to Damon, a couple of meters away. His face looks passive, but as though he's swallowing more than usual. I look around at our group, at our teachers and classmates, and each expression is harder, more shocked at their surroundings than before. Mrs. Scott's usually styled bob looks limp and lifeless; her shoulders sag like she's holding the weight of the world on her shoulders and her nails are so chapped and broken which I notice as she bites on them.

Once we have finished listening, we are assigned our jobs. I am given a job with Sophie and a handful of others, to sort through the piles of clothes that have been donated. Our job is to sort through and find the ones that are worth keeping or in good enough condition. They will be sent to refugee camps and given out to hotels and other places like the one we are in. Evan, Damon, and Tom along with a lot of others get the stereotypical job of clearing away as much as they can from the streets such as moving tree branches from doorways or the middle of the road and any removable rubble. Their team starts to work systematically to get the job done.

"So that's what's up then," Sophie says to me casually after ten minutes of filtering through the first pile of clothing. Some of it smells awful, some of the clothes have blood or stains on them and a majority of them are filthy and/or wet. A lady explains that these bags have been left out in the rain for days so that explains the wet ones. The group we are with keep to themselves for the most part, a lot of them much older than Sophie and me. They go through the clothes like they are on a mission and for the most part, remain silent. One girl has barely filtered through her first pile, each piece of clothing she carefully examines for a couple of minutes each.

"What are you talking about?" I respond, dumping a piece of ripped clothing into the bag that's labeled *Trash*.

"I mean you and Evan." She shrugs, but I can see she's dying to come out with something.

"There is no '*me and Evan*'," I tell her using air quotes. "You know that."

"I know that your dating is part of a larger plan," Sophie looks up at me and her lip curls, "but something's changed. It's not Evan versus Kayla anymore. It's Evan *and* Kayla." She tosses three shirts in the salvageable bag and shakes her head. I can't help but feel confused. *That's a good thing, right?*

As if she can read my thoughts, she carries on talking, "I'm not saying that it's a bad thing. I'm saying that it's the weirdest thing to be thrown in a situation where you're completely isolated from everyone. We haven't had any contact with our parents for nearly four weeks now. We have spent the majority of our time stuck in an airport and the only company we have had is each other." She pauses to get another pile of clothing.

"I'm just saying that this situation is so different to what we're used to and that people come together, and people grow apart. I just don't want you to get your hopes up. I don't want you to think that once we're home, you'll continue this...*friendship*. It might just be something that happened here and you both forget about it when we get home. I know you've spent an awful lot of time together for people who supposedly hate each other. I'm just worried your feelings are going to get hurt."

I think about what she says. "Hate is a strong word, and even if what we felt for each other was hate, I feel like Evan and I have at least mutually come to some conclusion that we don't anymore." I flick through my pile of clothing quickly, trying to distract my thoughts. "Evan has offered me a friendship with no strings. He didn't have to say it, he just proved it. I don't need to feel that I am expected to do anything or that he is in this for anything else, it kind of just works. He's stable. I don't need to worry about what he's going to do or say next. I don't really need to think about anything at all."

Sophie stops everything she does and throws her arm around my neck and I'm so surprised that I stumble back, knocking off my pile of clothing from the table. She's grinning from ear to ear and I can't help but smile back, it's kind of infectious. But it's also the sort of smile that says *I know something you don't*.

"Why are you hugging me?" I say into her chest.

"Because I'm happy." She lets me go and reaches for another shirt. This girl doesn't make any sense. She folds the shirt and tries to cover her smirk. "And soon you will be too."

"What makes you think I'm not happy?" I frown, reaching for my next clothing item but realizing they're all on the floor. I bend down to scoop the pile and chuck them on the counter. My hands are wet and muddy, and I have to wipe them on my jeans to clean them.

"Oh, no reason." She tosses a shirt in my direction and I fold it and put it in the salvage bag. "But I think when you're ready to commit again, you will realize that the happiness you really need has been dangling in front of you all of this time." She holds up a rag that's drenched in murky water and filth and waggles it in my face. It makes me laugh, despite the water particles getting on my arm and face.

"Hey, watch it," one of the girls says, wiping water off her nose. I recognize her from one of my AP classes back at home, Ellen or Ellie or something. Sophie and I giggle harder.

I don't know what Sophie means about commitment. Her words have always had a point of being ambiguous; she kind of lives off them. She has always had a fascination with books or movies that carry a handful of different meanings. She enjoys figuring them out. So much so, last summer she'd set herself a challenge to read every single thought-provoking book on a Goodreads list she had found, and the girl almost did it, two books and she would have been the happiest girl on earth.

So, I guess I kind of know what she is doing, she's setting me my own challenge—one I intend to follow.

Chapter Twenty-One

It has started to occur to me how much I really do miss home. I haven't heard my mom's voice for nearly four weeks. I haven't slept in my bed for almost that long as well, and despite her best efforts, Mrs. Scott's tireless efforts to try and get us all to call home has failed. It would cost us sixty-four euros each, around three hundred dollars and none of us have brought that kind of money with us. The disappointed look she gives us every time a new student asks makes my heart hurt for her. She thinks it's her responsibility and we all know there isn't anything she can do about it. She's trying her best but the lines are simply down, and the ones running are just too expensive.

I spend my day mostly helping people out. I dabble in cleaning and at the food bank and even get a chance to help in medical. I mostly give out Band-Aids and first aid kits to families and talk to the people who are there but it's something, and it's better than doing nothing. I feel like I'm making some kind of progress, and it makes me feel a little bit better.

Despite the fact Evan and I have agreed on alternate nights on the couch, I want nothing more than to be curled up in my own bed. There is no greater feeling than coming home from somewhere and flopping onto your sheets, feeling your mattress spring and your pillow curling around your head. I crave the feeling so much that every night I allow myself to imagine I'm there, in my bedroom with all my stuff scattered around me. I allow myself only the night to imagine, anything more and I think I will go crazy.

It's just before dinner and Damon is up in the room with Evan and me. He's been trying to get his cell phone to connect for ages, and he's the only one of us who still has theirs fully intact. Evan is cleaning—*I know*—and making a pile of dirty clothes at the foot of the bed. The floor has become an array of many things: socks, shoes, a fork; despite my best efforts to pick them up, I'm not Evan's maid.

But I'm antsy. And I always clean when I'm nervous because today isn't just any day, today is the day Adam leaves and I'm not sure if I'm ready to say goodbye. I have seen him a handful of times since the kiss from a distance. He's spent most of the time in a medical tent a couple of blocks away from the hotel and I can't deny him the fact of helping people to just speak to me. I also know he shouldn't mean as much to me as he does, but when someone quite literally saves your life and was your hero in a time of need, you kind of can't help the butterflies. I can't stop thinking about it as I fold some of my shirts into my case. In the weeks I have known Adam, he made me feel safe. I want nothing more than to repay him with the feeling of gratitude back. I don't know how long I have been consumed with thoughts, but a knock at the door makes them fade away as if they were never there.

I get up, toss my shirt on top of my suitcase and head to the door. I already know who it is before I answer and it's no surprise to see Adam standing there.

"Hey."

"Hey back." He smiles. "Should we go somewhere more private?"

"Uh, sure." I turn away from him to grab my jacket, shutting the door behind me.

"You good?"

"Yeah," I say slowly. "I'm good."

You know those moments where your heart literally falters as if it's not beating at all and your fingertips go tingly from the squeezing you can't help from doing? Well, that is this moment. I know that this walk is likely to be the last we will have, for a while at least.

"Just say it," I start. We find a place to sit within the hotel and Adam's got his arm flung across the back of the chairs, his knee incessantly shaking up and down. It's annoying, so I place my hand on it to stop him.

Adam finally looks to me, his green eyes wide though his expression is sullen. "Kayla."

"You're going back," I state the inevitable. My voice is harder and harsher than I mean, as if I'm spitting out the words. I know it's wrong. It's not his fault. I knew this was coming. "When do you leave?"

He closes his eyes and pulls me closer to him. We're lucky. It's near dinner time so everybody is either in their rooms or helping out in the kitchen. There is nobody here. As far as I know, Jess never spilled to Ben. I'm sure I'd have heard it by now if she did. I can feel Adam's chest rise and fall and I know this is hurting him too. It makes it harder to know that it's hurting him too.

"Tonight," he tells me. "Just after dinner."

"You leave in an hour." I let the thought sink in and squeeze my eyes closed. I know I'm no Dorothy or anything, but I'd do anything right now to tap my shoes three times and wish this isn't happening. I know this isn't love, my feelings for Adam are simple and straightforward and in no way represent the complexity of being in love, but I can't deny what is in front of me. The prospect of him going back to England to be shipped out to somewhere dangerous makes me feel sick with worry.

"I am being flown out by helicopter," Adam tells me and I nod, though it's like the world around me isn't quite in focus.

My thoughts are swirling so much that I don't notice that Adam is talking. And it isn't to me anymore; he's talking to a kid. I look up from

Adam's chest and see the boy we saved back at the airport is grinning ear-to-ear, an ice pop in his hand. I don't catch the conversation, but it seems as if he is going home and that means there's hope for us all.

"Good luck man," Adam says and gives the boy a high five. The boy looks over at me and holds his hand out, ready for me to high five him too. I do, it makes me wake up from my mind.

"Glad you're doing well now," I say to him. He licks his ice pop and then turns, running back to his mother with a wave. It's not much, but it makes me smile.

I've never been the type of person who insists on being remembered, but maybe in thirty years' time when that kid has his own children and he might suffer another allergic reaction, he will remember this moment in that airport where two seemingly uninterested strangers work together to help save his life. Maybe he won't ever think of it again. Maybe the details will become foggy and the whole situation will become one mess that he can't solve. Maybe that's okay. Maybe I'm alright with that too.

But I'm not sure what to feel about Adam leaving. Part of me wants to beg him to stay and to come back to the US and do some medical training there. I think about all the possibilities a trained surgeon could do in the field. The other part of me wants to let him go. His life is a map that didn't include me as a destination, and I don't want to be that type of girl who lets the person they care about give up on something they're truly passionate and great at. So, I don't say anything else to Adam. I take his hand and we walk back to his room and I spend the last hour with him laughing and talking about different things. It's nice; it feels warm and calm and I realize then that Adam was the calm *after* the storm. He might not have been there before everything happened, but he was there after.

•　　　•　　　•

"We missed you at dinner." Evan flops onto his bed, his towel dried hair spraying water all over me.

"Well, that's a lie." I laugh. "I doubt my presence was *that* missed." But my stomach rumbles in protest. I miss dinner.

"Don't doubt my connection to you, Kayla." Evan tosses his towel at me and places his hand to his heart. "We are one and forever."

"Shut up." I laugh.

"Hey!" He grabs the cushion he has been lying on and throws it at me.

"Don't start this shit again," I warn him. "I'm not in the mood. Tonight, I require sleep, lots and lots of it, and maybe even a hot chocolate."

"Well, considering hot chocolate is definitely off the menu, sleep is the only thing you're gonna get." He stands and slips a shirt over his head. "You can sleep here if you want. I can see you keep waking up with a backache."

"Aw," I purr and throw the very cushion he threw at me his way. "Are you really taking my feelings into account? I think I'm witnessing a new man being born here."

"Don't be an idiot. I'm being a gentleman." He pulls the duvet out and I realize he means besides him and not alone.

"I'll sleep here if you promise me two things." I raise an eyebrow at him.

"And what are those, your majesty?" He gets into bed and fiddles with his pillow. I arch an eyebrow as he gets comfy and climb into the bed on the other side.

"One: you don't snore. I can't be dealing with it, I'm shattered." I adjust my own pillow so that I'm comfy.

"Has anyone ever told you that you are very high maintenance?" Evan smirks and flips over on the bed and rests his chin in his hand, looking at me expectantly. "And what's the second thing?"

"I swear to God if I wake up with you cuddling me, this here," I point to the middle of the bed, "will contain a wall. This friendship of ours doesn't need a dose of benefits, okay?"

"That's fine by me, *your majesty.*"

I flop down on my side of the bed and frown. "And the third thing."

Evan rolls his eyes, teasing. "Kayla, you only said two rules."

I turn on my side. "Well, this one is very important."

"Go on."

"Don't ever call me *your majesty* again. I'm not a princess and I certainly don't act like one."

I hear Evan's snort of disagreement from the other side of the bed and then a low mumble, "Deal."

Chapter Twenty-Two

Someone knocks on the door that night, or morning—depending on how you classify 2 am. I'm in deep sleep, my dreaming interrupted by the breathing of a male who snores too loudly and smells too naturally musky, enough that it makes you cough.

I poke Evan to wake him, my hand shooting out of the pillow wall for him to go and see who it is, though his reply is a muffled grunt because his head is pressed into the pillow. I turn to my right side and poke him again. His bare skin is hot, and I feel him relax under my touch. His skin reacts and goosebumps form under my fingers.

"Evan!" I whisper-shout, patting him on the back. "Go and get the door," I command.

"Piss off," he mutters into his pillow and turns so that he isn't facing me anymore. "You go and get it."

"What if it's someone here to kill us?" I exaggerate, though it is a worry. I break the pillow wall so that I can poke him again. "You're the guy."

"And here's me thinking you're all about equality," he shifts again, "way to stereotype someone."

"Oh, for Christ sake!" I push myself up and rub my head, my eyes sore. "If you hear me scream then it's on you."

"Whatever." He flaps his hand in my direction, but I'm sitting up and he touches my boob by accident. For a long second, both of us freeze. I look down at his hand which hasn't moved from my boob. It's awkward and I press my lips together.

"Excuse me." I look over at him. "Your hand needs to return to its assigned seat."

"Right." Evan sleepily moves his hand and drops it to the broken pillow wall. I don't move for another moment; the knocking has stopped and instead I hear heavy breathing from the other side of the door. It's the perfect set up to get murdered.

I am going to die.

"The door," Evan prompts when I don't move.

Right, of course. I get up, my shirt rising, and I push it down before Evan can open his eyes and catch a glimpse of anything else I don't want him to see. The knocking starts again, and I fling the door open, my body suddenly bombarded by another body. I don't have the energy to scream.

"*Oh my God,* I thought you'd been murdered or something. Did you not hear me knocking?" Sophie's arms wrap tighter around my shoulders and then she pulls me out of her hug, staring me down. She's wearing a weird combination of her PJ top and a pair of jeans. It looks as if she's gotten dressed in the dark.

"It's fucking two in the morning." I blink at her. "I'm not inclined to open the door to possible killers at this time of night."

"Morning," Sophie corrects and winks. "And I'm not a killer."

"I know, whatever." I open the door wider, so she can come in and head back towards the bedroom in search of more sleep. "What the hell is so urgent that you have to come knocking in the early hours of the morning for? If it's something trivial, Sophie, then I will be the one doing the killing."

"You're not going to believe it," Sophie starts, her face lighting up with a smile.

"Well, I won't know what to believe unless you spit it out," I respond, my voice grumpy from the lack of sleep. She doesn't notice it though, or if she does, she ignores it.

She frowns as she sees Evan lying in the bed, the pillow wall dismantled and the other side clearly there for me. Her eyes divert from the bed and then turn to me, then back to Evan again, and she opens her mouth as if she's about to say something but thinks better of it.

"She's done it! Mrs. Scott has got us a plane."

"She's what?" But it isn't me saying it, it's Evan.

"To make it short." Sophie flops down on the end of the bed and rolls out. She's tall and her legs are so long that they dangle off the edge. "We're going home, baby!"

•   •   •

As much as I am desperate to get home, to shower in my own bathroom, to sleep in my own bed and to see my mom, a part of me doesn't want to leave. I see Sophie standing across from me in the foyer, helping another girl out with her suitcase that's toppled over. Damon is with her and they're both in deep conversation about something as Sophie struggles with the girl to get her suitcase upright. I know that the girl Sophie is helping is one of those who were able to retrieve her belongings, not everyone was as lucky, and people have been sharing the clothes they have. I think about what Sophie said a couple of days ago, about how being at home might just be *home* and that this thing between Evan and me, this friendship or mutual bond we have gained, might not be the same. It pains me to think about it, about losing Evan. I don't want to lose anyone else. I don't want anything else to change. I feel like I have already lost enough this trip.

Evan holds my hand in front of everyone and it has sort of become instinctive now for me to lean against him or hold his hand back—small bits of affection for show. I can see Ben and Jess in the corner and I can feel them both watching which makes me turn to Evan and plant a small kiss on his cheek. Evan looks amazed for a moment, but quickly recovers and grins and I cannot tell if it's genuine or not.

The ride to the airfield where the plane is meeting us is mostly silent. Nobody has much of anything to say and the excitement has either worn off, or people are waiting until we are actually in the air to feel like it's real. Anything could happen from here to the plane. Nothing seems too far-fetched anymore.

Evan and I are both quiet. We have chosen to sit together despite not communicating it between ourselves and I don't mind, he's my friend. He has his arm thrown over my shoulder and is rubbing the tip of my arm subconsciously. It feels nice. This whole thing between us feels nice, too nice for what it's supposed to be, which makes me dread going home even more. I don't want it to end. But I can't help thinking that as everyone says goodbye to the people they have met, our goodbye isn't to everyone else; it's to each other. I'm conscious of the fact that Ben is staring. He's a couple of rows back on the opposite side of the coach but he has a good view. He's been staring the whole time. He's got his earphones on, but we all know there is no way in hell he's listening to anything. I try to avoid staring back and turn in towards Evan, who smiles down at me.

"I know," he murmurs. "I see him too."

"So, it worked," I reply. "He's jealous."

"It has been working long before this," Evan barely opens his mouth when he speaks. I frown up at him and twist, so I can see him better. I don't get what he means. I've barely laid my eyes on Ben in the last couple of days.

"What do you mean?" I ask.

"I mean he cornered me the other night, asked if my intentions were good and wanted to know *all* the details," Evan subtly chuckles, "because all of his intentions have been stellar."

This takes me by surprise. "What did he say exactly?" I try not to sound too curious, but I can't quite work out if I'm curious about what Evan said or what Ben asked.

"He tried to trick me you know, asked if I knew why you never wear shorter tops. I wasn't sure if he asked this particular question to know if we'd slept together yet or if I knew you. He seems to think I'm stupid, that I wouldn't know about your birthmark." Evan shakes his head and taps his foot on the floor. "He is obviously wrong."

I'm taken back. "Wait, *you* know about my birthmark?" I look down at myself, consciously moving my hand towards the bottom of my stomach.

"Of course, I know about your birthmark." Evan looks at me quizzically, like I'm out of my mind by suggesting he didn't know about this like it is tattooed on my forehead. "I know that it's in the shape of a funny circle and you've been self-conscious about it since you knew that it is really visible. You don't wear short tops because you hate the way the tip of it sticks out of your pants and in some lights, it looks like a patch of bad fake tan."

I let out a sharp breath and drop my hand. "When have you ever seen it?"

He gives me a look that reads *you've got to be joking.* "We've been neighbors for years, Kayla. Your bedroom is directly across from mine."

Jesus Christ, what else has he seen?

I purse my lips in curiosity, my mind wandering back to when I would've stood near my rear window with my birthmark showing. I come up blank. "I just didn't think you would have…" I trail off. Notice isn't the right word because I always made sure Evan knew I was there, waiting for the next moment to annoy him. But he had noticed me, he sees me.

"Noticed? You're pretty hard to miss."

I know he doesn't mean it in the way I want him to mean it, but it makes my heart squeeze and I'm left holding my breath. I try to change the subject. "So, Ben believes it?" I reconfirm.

"He better believe it." Evan snorts. "I basically made some love declaration in front of him; it was right up your alley, would've loved it."

"Love declaration?" I question.

"Yeah, a speech about love." He stops rubbing my arm and taps at it with the tips of his fingers instead. This feels less nice and more *annoying* and I try and shake off the feeling that keeps stirring the pit of my stomach.

"Well, don't push it," I say slowly. "I don't think it happens that fast."

"We'll see." He smiles.

I have no idea what he means by this, or whether it means anything because of course, I overthink pretty much everything.

I pull away from him as we arrive at the airfield. My stomach is jittery from thinking too much so I decide to redirect my thoughts to going home, to seeing my family. I turn to look over my shoulder and Tom's behind us, beaming.

He reads a back of the book he is holding. "In the wake of a tragedy, good always comes." I laugh, and Tom reaches over the seat to smack Evan's back playfully. "You ready for this FIFA game?"

Evan chuckles, leaving me to join his friend's conversation. "I'm beyond ready."

Chapter Twenty-Three

It's safe to say I am scared to go on the plane.

And I don't mean in the literal sense that I'm scared we are going to crash, though the thought of it is troubling. I'm scared that leaving Italy is like leaving a major part of my life behind. I can't quite put my finger on it, but there is something scary about leaving behind this entire experience. I feel like I have lost and gained so much in the process. It was the worst but best time of my life.

Evan, on the other hand, is as closed as a book. He hasn't expressed any emotion about going home, almost as if he's dreading walking through the doors. He's also spent the majority of the time muttering in a low voice with Tom whose face looks strained like they are having a conversation he doesn't like. Sophie's off with a girl she became close with after room sharing, and while I don't mind having this time alone to think, I look awkward just standing here.

We're all crowded around the tarmac of the runway, waiting for the tank to fuel up and the pilot to be ready. I spot Jess through the crowd of students standing alone by the crook of the plane. She looks miserable; her hair is pulled back into a messy bun though most of it is falling out like her elastic is too small. She's got the type of look on her face that makes me think something has happened between her and Ben.

I wish I could stop myself, but something inside me compels me to go over to her. Maybe it's the fact that she looks so sad and something in me feels kind of bad for her despite everything. If it's Ben related, I feel for her, I know what it's like. Somehow, I find myself walking her way. She notices me just as I reach her, and I watch as she grimaces as if she's repulsed to see me. I kind of want to turn back around and not even bother.

"Come to gloat?" she says with a snide tone. Another chunk of hair comes dangling down from her bun. "Because if you are, I'll save my breath and tell you to piss off now."

"I haven't come to gloat," I tell her truthfully but make a face. "In fact, if I told you anything, the best advice I could give you is that you're free. Ben isn't a future. He's a *for now* kind of boy. He doesn't actually scream someone you could see yourself marrying and having children with…" I trail off and shrug my shoulders. "To be honest, looking back, those thoughts never once crossed my mind. So, Jess, maybe you did me a favor."

"I'd say you're welcome if I really thought you meant it," she replies, but her eyes are studying me, and I know she's thinking about what I've said. She knows I mean it. She's considering it herself.

"I do mean it," I shift on my feet and shrug, "but hey, you already knew that before I had to open my mouth."

She pauses for a moment and doesn't say anything. She's looking past my shoulder, at someone else and then her eyes drop back to me. "You really love him, don't you?"

I'm about to spin around and turn back, frowning. "Ben? Nope. I don't have any feelings for him whatsoever, not really—"

"I meant Evan," she cuts me off.

"Oh." I'm a little taken back. *Love him?* We're only just friends.

"So, do you?" she questions. "Love him?"

I look at her carefully, trying to judge if this is a trick question or not. "Um, if I'm honest, I don't know what I feel."

"Well, that makes one of you," Jess crosses her arms and gives me a look. "He hasn't been able to take his eyes off you since we've been here." I hear a grunt in her voice, but she also sounds genuine. I guess she's been watching us and our *acting* is better than we thought.

"What are you talking about?" This comes out automatically and for a moment, I forgot Evan and I are pretending to date.

Jess narrows her eyes. "You are joking right? It's literally the weirdest thing I've ever seen. You are his main priority; he's always watching to make sure nobody's talking shit about you or making sure you're okay. That day back in the airport when you got badly hurt, he was by your side morning, noon, and night. He made sure your leg got better. I saw him a couple of days before you announced you were together and he was talking about you to this group of guys. I didn't hear the gist of the conversation, but he was definitely defending you. I've never once seen him like this." She tosses her ponytail behind her head. *"Ever."*

I'm filled with a feeling I haven't recognized before and it's startling. It's the kind of feeling you get when you first hear a firework go off and you aren't expecting the loud noise. I take a deep breath, feeling slightly winded from what she has just said but don't get much more time to process because I can hear Mrs. Scott's voice over the booming noise of another plane taking off, just as she's directing us to the plane's doors. It's time.

When I look back to respond to Jess, she's already gone, her blonde ponytail bobbing in the wind.

"You coming?" It's Evan holding out his hand and I look up to see half a dozen people staring.

"I'm coming."

• • •

This plane ride home isn't like the one we had when we arrived. For one, I'm not sitting next to someone I can barely stand, and for another, there are zero comfy seats. It's one of those planes that hasn't been used in decades and therefore, the chairs smell and I can feel every single hit of wind like I'm flying in the sky myself. Susy Donavon, chronic nail picker, is also across the aisle from Evan and me again and this time does not have the room to be intently picking at her toenails.

"She said something to you, didn't she?" Evan's beside me, and since take off we haven't said one word to each other.

"She didn't have to," I mumble. It's a half-lie.

"What's that supposed to mean?"

"Nothing." I dismiss his pushing because I don't feel like I want to get into it right now. I don't have the energy. But I'm also not sure what I would say, *hey, so Jess thinks you have feelings for me.*

Yeah, no.

I stare out the window and look down below, but I can't see anything through the thick covering of the clouds, so I'm essentially staring at nothing. I still gaze nevertheless and fidget in my seat for distraction. I can feel the heat of Evan's gaze on my back, and I try to ignore it. I know he's worried.

"Kayla," Evan prompts after a while. "Are you bored?" I raise an eyebrow at the window before realizing he can't see it.

I swivel in my chair, losing my comfy position, and cock my head slightly. "What?"

"I asked if you were bored." Evan shrugs and pulls out a notepad from the compartment in front "Do you have a pen?" he asks.

"Uh, yeah," I stammer and reach into my bag to find a miscellaneous pen. I hand it to him and watch him draw out a funny looking grid and he writes MASH in capital letters on the top of the page.

"This is a game my sister showed me," he explains, smoothing out my confusion. "She taught it to me just before we left, said it's what all the kids are doing now." Evan's sister is the same age as my brother, ten years old, and from what I can remember it looks similar to something my own brother showed me a while ago, so I nod.

"Okay, so what do we have to do?"

"I have to ask you some questions first," he says and draws three little dashes on one side of the grid. "Okay, pick three guy names, they can be random or whatever."

"Oh, uh. Jack, Henry, and Ethan," I tell him, spouting off names from the top of my head. Evan writes the names next to each dash and then looks at me.

"You're not very inventive," he comments. "I was thinking more along the lines of Ernest, Matthew, and Phillipe."

"Well, you didn't give me much time to pick," I defend, shaking my head. "Now what do I have to do?"

"Name three jobs you would like to have and three jobs you wouldn't want to have," he says and draws six dashes along another side of the grid.

"Um, good jobs…I guess would be like a journalist for a good magazine, maybe a teacher—I guess I've always liked working with kids, and *oh*, the president or maybe even the first lady. You can do a little slash between those two as they're pretty much the same," I ramble. "In terms of shitty jobs, well obviously someone who picks up trash, or…"

And the game goes on like that. Evan and I spend the whole time playing this MASH game which apparently determines your future. After he had asked me several questions about how much money I would earn and what type of house I would be in and how many children I would have, he began crossing off the dashes. My first result ended up being a mother of twelve kids who owned a Porsche whilst living in a garage. Her job was the President of the United States though. So you could see how this game isn't exactly reliable.

Evan falls asleep at some point, his head lolling on my shoulder and his palm on my knee. It had dropped from his lap at some point during the flight, but I don't want to move it without risking waking him up. The guy needed to sleep, hell I did too. I just can't. I'm so excited to get home. I can't stop thinking about the first thing I am going to do when I get in.

It's hours later when I decide to wake him up as the seatbelt sign turns back on and a bundle of students rush to return to their seats. The excitement of being back in American air stirs something inside of me and I run my hand along Evan's cheek, shaking him slightly to wake him.

"Hey, Winters," I whisper. "You're going to want to wake up for this."

His eyes blink open and he sits up, grimacing as he rubs his neck. "How long have I been asleep?"

"A couple of hours," I tell him.

"And you let me sleep on your shoulder? How adorable, I guess the roles are reversed," Evan teases, rubbing his eyes.

I smack him. "Just because we're back on American soil, doesn't mean you can go back to being a jerk."

He laughs and moves closer to get a better look outside the window. I can see the night lights of our brilliant city, the houses and the roads. I smile, the grin going so high that I can feel it bursting through the top of the plane. Three and a half weeks ago, I left this place thinking I was getting away for a long weekend with my classmates. But being stranded in an airport and encountering more than enough near-death experiences, I think that I've learned that you have one shot at life. Take it or lose it. Either way, it's fleeting. You're not going to get another one.

"It's so weird to be back," Evan murmurs in my ear, "to see it all again. The lights, the cars, the *familiarity*. It's like we never left."

I grin deeper. "That's the funny thing," I murmur back. "That's what it's supposed to feel like to be home."

Chapter Twenty-Four

Two weeks after arriving home, I've seen my friends a grand total of zero times, unless you count the one occasion I saw Evan. In fact, the only person I've seen more than once is my mom, who has taken up the incessant need to check on me every three seconds. The first, (and apparently last) time I saw Evan was when his mom dragged him out of his own room to go grocery shopping. I only know this information because I could see his mom load her shopping tote into the car and Evan stumble in with her. I had pretty much begged Mom to go to Target to collect some bits I had supposedly been missing because I wanted to run into him. I had seen Evan at the counter and we smiled—*smiled* like we were acquaintances. I pretty much cursed myself the entire ride home, kicking myself for being the girl who goes somewhere just because a boy is there. And it angers me that Sophie is right, it's like nothing has ever happened. Home is the same.

Sophie.

My best friend had been trying to message me on my laptop for days now. Since misplacing my phone in Italy, I have been waiting for a new one to come in the post courtesy of my phone company after what we went through. After her eighth message, I had told her I was spending time with family this week, and that I would see her next week when we would be attending a memorial at school with the rest of our classmates so we could recognize the people who died in Italy. It is something I haven't even decided whether to go to or not.

"Honey." It's Mom again. She knocks on my door and opens it, peering around the corner. "Kayla, you need to get up." She walks into my room and opens my curtains, letting in beads of bright light that I haven't encountered for days.

"Mom!" I yell, sitting up from the same position I have found myself in for hours.

"Kayla, for God's sake, this is getting ridiculous!" She tries to sound sincere, but her voice wobbles and her face is a picture of defeat. "I can't stand seeing you like this."

"Seeing me like what? I'm fine!" Frustrated, I flop back down onto my bed and turn over, hoping she will get the message and leave. I just need to wallow, I need to be alone. *Why does nobody understand that I can be sick and not show any physical symptoms?*

"You can't live like this, honey," she murmurs after a long period of silence. "It's not healthy. You need to talk to someone about it and I mean *really* talk Kayla, not sit there in silence in your therapy sessions. What you went through was traumatic."

"Mom, please," I say, muffled by the pillow in front of me. I don't see how talking to someone about something they can't relate to will help me. My therapist wasn't with me when this happened; she wasn't hurt, she didn't see dead bodies.

"At least take a shower, baby." She reaches over to touch me and my automatic reaction is to flinch. "It reeks in here."

But I don't shower, not even after she leaves.

•   •   •

The wind isn't very strong, but it's freezing and my legs fidget on my mattress, my body is awake and my mind is unable to rest. My window has stayed open all week since arriving back home, the desperate need for fresh air is overwhelming. I feel confined without it open. Since being back in my own surroundings, I feel like a sitting duck, like I am waiting for something bad to happen. I'm also ridiculously jumpy. The sound of the trash being taken in the morning makes me fly out of bed and towards my window. My dog scratching against my door to come in, a car starting. I feel on edge constantly.

It's so cold and I have no choice but to pull myself out of bed and try and close the window instead of just pulling on another layer of clothing. My legs are weak as I stumble across the short walk from my bed to the left window. Once I get there, I debate whether to shut it or not.

"Hey," I hear. It's a little louder than a whisper but couldn't really be called a voice.

I snap my head behind me, my hairline just brushing the window pane. My body goes on alert, automatically checking for creepy strangers lurking in the depths of my dark bedroom. There is no one there. I shake my head. I have been on high alert a lot since returning. But it's when I turn again to pull my window shut that the whisper comes again.

"*Kayla*." I realize now that the voice isn't behind me, it's in front of me—coming out of Evan's bathroom window to be precise.

"Evan?" I squint in the darkness and lean closer out of the window so I can see if it's him. I wouldn't exactly know who else it could be.

"No, it's the devil." Evan chuckles back. I can't see him at all, only the open bathroom window and a figure looming on the other side of it.

"So *you*, then," I retort, my mood lifting.

"Ouch." He feigns a heartache as I see his silhouette move so his hand presses against his chest. "You do hurt me, Kayla Burns."

I laugh a little bit. "I do aim to please." The space between our houses falls silent again. I can hear the familiarity of the crickets coating the grass and the sound of cars driving past our road and onto the busy streets. "I feel like I haven't spoken to you in ages," I start saying, though I'm not a hundred percent sure he's still there.

"I know, me too," Evan agrees. "I guess it's weird. We spent a little over three weeks in each other's company and suddenly we have been thrust out of the bubble everyone was in. I haven't really had a chance to sit and think about it all."

"Have you been going to the sessions?" I ask.

The school has made our entire senior class have at least two sessions a week with a therapist they brought in from Michigan who specializes in adolescents and the PTSD of disasters. She spent the whole session I attended on Friday talking about my accident. I kept telling her I didn't remember anything, and it's true, most of what I remember is from what other people have told me. Though, this didn't stop her making sure I was attending my physio sessions the hospital is making me have. They had said from the resources and Adam's knowledge, I am lucky to still have my leg and not have caught an infection. I guess in some ways, I have been lucky, I just wish now I could *feel* it.

"I can't really hear you," Evan says through the darkness. "Wait, I'm coming over."

"Wait, you're what?" I look down at my outfit and grimace. I'm wearing an oversized Care Bears shirt I've been wearing for days and no bra. I forgot to brush my teeth today and my hair hasn't been washed. I'm a state and even though I know he has seen me worse, injured and bloody, I can't help but grimace.

Evan's climbing over the tree with skilled precision and moves so that he swings on another branch that connects to my window pane. It's too late for him to turn back now, so I let him in with a grunt.

"Make yourself at home," I mutter sarcastically.

Evan picks up on this and smiles as he wipes his hands down on the back of his jeans. "Thanks," he says, and he flops onto my bed.

"Whate—"

"—are you wearing a Care Bears shirt?" he interrupts me and pouts slightly as if he's about to laugh.

"What, oh, you mean this old thing," I dismiss. "Well, I mean I didn't have anything else clean so…" I trail off.

"Right." Evan gives me a look. "I believe you."

"I don't need you to believe me," I tell him. "It doesn't matter what I wear. I wasn't exactly expecting company," I explain, defensive. I sit on the end of my bed and rub my eyes. I'm exhausted. Staring at the same wall for hours does make you tired.

"You aren't sleeping, are you?" It's less of a question and more of a statement. Evan sits up, pushes forward so that he is right behind me. I don't move, though my chest makes excessive heaves as my breathing picks up. I can feel his chest on my back and his legs droop down beside mine.

"Why would you say that?" I murmur. "Do I really look that bad?"

"Of course not," he says quickly. "But I know what it feels like," he continues. Evan doesn't give me enough to time to ask him what he means before he speaks again, "To be here when there is still chaos in Italy. I know the feeling of getting into a bed when you have seen firsthand what many people don't have anymore."

"You haven't been sleeping either." It's another statement that's made, one Evan doesn't deny.

"No." He breathes out heavily. "No, I haven't."

"I wish it would stop," I tell him.

He touches the bottom of my neck with the palm of his hand. It's exactly the part where my shoulder connects. His hands are warm and I fight the urge to lean my head into his palm. "What do you want to stop?"

I shrug. "This guilty feeling. I was so wrapped up with going home that I barely spared a thought for all of the people I was leaving behind."

"Adam, you mean." Evan's voice is rough.

"Yes, Adam," I tell him truthfully. "But also all of the people we met there. The people who helped save me, save *all* of us."

"I think about it too," Evan says honestly. "But I also think about everything else that's happened. I think about the fact we tried our best to help the people there. I might have only been equipped with a reckless plan and a class full of seniors to make happy, but if we hadn't found a way to the main part of the airport, we'd all be dead. So yes, I feel guilty as hell for leaving everyone else behind, but I'm also proud of myself for making sure that I tried to keep our class alive. I know I didn't sit and do nothing." Evan leans his head on my shoulder and wraps his arm around my stomach, pulling me closer. I'm startled by his sudden affection and it takes me a moment to process what's happening. But I want it.

"That's one way to look at it," I whisper.

"It's the *only* way, Kayla," Evan replies.

"So what now?" I say after a while of silence. Truthfully, I could've fallen asleep right here, right now. My eyes are droopy and my body is relaxed. I just want to grab a blanket and wrap it around myself.

Evan chuckles slightly as if this was the last thing he was expecting me to say. "Now we sleep." He doesn't have to tell me twice.

Chapter Twenty-Five

To say I was in a predicament I didn't expect to be in at nine o'clock this morning would have been an understatement. At the least, it wasn't all my fault. I didn't expect to be lining up in a club's restroom holding back my best friend's hair while she emptied the contents of her alcohol binge. I also didn't expect for Evan Winters to be here, raging drunk with his friends and kissing said friend before she was about to puke. But then again, this morning it didn't even occur to me this situation would happen. I was neither in the mood to go out anywhere or expect that I would *ever* gain this stomach punching jealousy in the pit of my stomach over a guy who I'd always referred to his name with the middle finger.

But I'm here, blaming myself for drinking too much to gain a flowing thought and the beatings of cheap booze already taking effect on my body. I might not have expected this sort of thing to happen at nine o'clock this morning, but then I also didn't think it was possible for me to intoxicatedly tell Evan Winters I really loved him and him to not even hear over the screams of what this club called their music.

But then again, I guess to know what I truly mean, we're going to have to start from the beginning.

Ten hours earlier…

Waking up alongside Evan Winters was just like the night in Rome I slept side by side with him. He is a bed hogger. He kicks and he has this spasm in his hand that makes him make jerky movements every so often. It's super annoying and kind of funny to watch all at once. He certainly isn't one for quiet sleeping. But he also doesn't try to be. There just isn't any bullshit with him. Once or twice I could feel him reach for me and each time it made me freeze, not sure if he was aware of what he was doing. Each time I had pulled away just in case he woke up and freaked that we were cuddling. But his head would reach out and snake around my waist, aimlessly rubbing at the skin from where my shirt had risen.

I woke up with my limbs curled to my sides and with my blanket thrown halfway across the room despite it being cold enough to be wrapped up in two. I try to ignore the fact I'm freezing and pull at the sheet to cover my legs and roll over. I keep my eyes shut, press deeper into my pillow and try to list the things I am grateful for. My therapist insisted I should do this every morning, so I started off on a good note. So far, it's not worked. I feel as shit as ever.

But I try.

1. I am grateful for being alive. Alive being the objective word. Yes, I am breathing, but alive? I wasn't exactly the sort of optimistic, getting-the-most-out-of-life kind of girl at the moment.

2. I survived a storm. The type of storm you tell your grandchildren about when you're ninety and by that time, I'll hopefully be kicking back in my hovering electric chair with a mug of tea.

3. I made friends with an enemy.

4. I found out the truth about my boyfriend.

5. I acted on a revenge plot that landed me in jail. Another crazy story to tell my grandchildren in my hover chair.

"You're doing it again," Evan's voice mutters from the middle of the bed because he doesn't have any concepts of sides.

"And what will that be?" I question, turning over, trying to act sleepy but I've been awake for a while.

"Thinking too much," he responds instantly.

"Well, someone's got to make up for the lack of thinking you do," I tease and kick his leg playfully. He makes a grunt type noise and faces me.

"You don't have to be so mean."

"I'm not being mean," I tell him. "I just choose when to be nice to you."

Evan chuckles and turns over some more so that his face is quite literally squashed into the crook of my arm. The pillow curls over his head so the only thing I see is his matted hair. "You smell quite nice for a girl who doesn't shower very often."

"Excuse me?"

"I heard your mom earlier," he explains, and then kicks his leg out of the sheet and points it towards the window. It's still open. He must have heard.

"Oh."

"It's fine. You smell sort of musky."

"Thank you," I shake my head. It's exactly what I think he smells like.

Evan rolls over and sits up. His back muscles tense underneath his shirt and I don't even let myself feel guilty for looking. Friends notice things about other friends, right? I'm purely observant. I notice how stunning Sophie is and how Tom really ought to go into modeling and how Damon is quick-witted and always wants to solve problems.

"I better be going," he murmurs.

"Oh, don't tell me you're one of *those* guys." I laugh and pick up the blanket that fell on the floor from the ground with my hand and wrap it around myself.

"Well, we are in quite a weird situation." Evan looks over his shoulder at me and smirks. "I'm not saying this isn't one I haven't been in before, but…" he trails off.

"Don't ruin it!" I smack his arm with the pillow he had been lying on.

He chuckles again, dodging my throw and walks towards the window. "Don't start that again." He grins as he pulls the window open wider.

"Oh and Kayla?" I look up at him expectantly and he looks even better in this light. His stubble is sexy and his hair is all rugged and cute at the same time.

"Yeah?"

"Happy birthday." But he's already outside the window before I can ask him how the hell he knows.

•   •   •

"I'm getting you drunk," it's a statement that Sophie says to me without any room for negotiation. She's sitting on the edge of my window and pushes the window wider to get some fresh air. I look at her through my damp hair that I have been brushing for too long and shake my head, most of my hair has now collected in my hairbrush. It feels good to be clean.

"I'm not in the mood," I tell her. "And I don't drink."

"You're eighteen Kayla," she tells me as if I am unaware of the age I have turned today. "It's time that you live a little. You've spent weeks locking yourself in this…*smelly* pit with old clothing and limited fresh air. Slap some makeup on, get yourself into a dress and forget about the world." Sophie jumps onto the end of my bed and laughs as she falls, crashing into the mound of blankets she has kicked off of me when she first arrived. Apparently, Mom had called her in a bid to get me out of bed on my birthday. The only thing that had worked was sending me into my bathroom for a shower. I really did smell.

"Soph—"

"—don't *'Soph'* me." She raises her head from the blankets and raises an eyebrow. "I have been waiting for this day since my birthday to take you out properly. You need a change of scenery and I totally can get us into a club."

"A change of scenery is going downstairs or even if I felt like pushing myself, maybe out for dinner." I shrug and pull my wet hair into a ponytail. "A change of scenery isn't going to a nightclub we will, no way in hell, get into and getting blitzed drunk. That's a freaking change of lifestyle."

Sophie rolls her eyes. "Do you know what your problem is?" she asks me.

"And what would that be?" I answer her, genuinely curious to see what she could possibly say that I didn't already know.

"You're scared. You don't take risks. And it's not because you don't want to, but you're afraid of the outcome. You think people are going to get hurt, or even worse—they'll hurt you. You're not afraid of alcohol Kayla, you're scared of what you might do when you're under its influence. You don't want it to show the real you." She folds her arms and kicks her legs out so that they scoot past my waist slightly.

Maybe it's what Sophie says that makes me want to go out. But in truth—despite the fact that all of my body is telling me she is right—she knows me better than I know myself. I have the desperate urge to make her feel like she is wrong. A sip of alcohol isn't going to send me into the real me, despite the thought looping my mind of *what if it does?*

"Fine," I nod my head. "We can go out, but call the others."

Sophie sits up, grinning. The sort of grin that says *purrrrleaseee.* "Oh, babe, it's already done."

Chapter Twenty-Six

The night started off something a bit like this: I'm chugging back my fifth shot of the night, Sophie beside me on the bar trying to discount our next round of drinks with the barman who has flashed her suggestive looks all night. My head is at the place where I don't feel at *all* drunk, but I know that it would be a terrible idea for me to drive home in the in-between stage I am at.

One of Justin Bieber's new songs is booming from the DJ who has been remixing all night. I've got my head resting on my shoulder, observing my surroundings. Sophie has asked some of the girls we are friendly with to come out and they beckon me over with huge smiles on their faces. I know that I'm not one to party, but we are all having such a good night that I kind of forget about the slump I had been in since we got back from Rome.

Sophie shakily brings our drinks over, chugging most of it down herself so that by the time she slammed the glasses on the table, the majority of it is soaking the floor instead of in the glass. Nobody seems to mind too much and we all collect our respected drinks, resuming our conversations. Miraculously, we have managed to get in. Sophie works her magic like I have never seen before. I watch my best friend stand up and she gives me the only look I have been avoiding all night. She wants me to dance.

"No."

"You don't even know what I was going to say!" She defends, putting down her purse.

"I do, and no I don't want to."

"It's your birthday, Kayla, you have to dance."

I shake my head, sighing. "I can't dance. I've definitely not drunk enough for that!"

Sophie puts a hand on her hip. "Nobody has to be drunk to dance!"

"Fine," I tell her and stand up, dropping my own stuff next to the girls. Sophie looks at me curiously and frowns, moving so that she blocks me getting out of my seat.

"Fine?" she repeats.

"Yes, *fine.*"

"Well, that didn't take much persuading." She steps back so I can get through and loops her arm around mine.

"I realize that I shouldn't need persuading," I tell her loudly over the noise. "I should just go for it." I'm not sure if Sophie hears me because she doesn't say anything back, just grins as her favorite song comes on just as we enter the flow of meshed bodies that they call the dance floor.

"I luuurrrve this song!" she chants over the beat of the music. The remix of the pop song is loud and shakes the ground as we struggle to find a space in the pit of bodies. I find myself apologizing to lots of people, despite them not caring or hearing. I can feel myself panic as Sophie finds a big enough spot that we can move without bashing into the next human being and she begins dancing. I watch her for what feels like ages. Her confidence is definitely attractive. She knows it, the guy looking at her knows it, and I know it too. I just wish I am more like her, carefree and confident.

The beat drops and suddenly I find myself jumping to the beat of the music just like everyone else. It's insane, the feeling alcohol gives you. My skirt loosens slightly around my waist and my hair flies so much over my face that I stop moving it away. I feel the alcohol dripping through my blood, fuelling my body like a match and a flame. I can feel my body tingling at the sensation of the dancing freely, the feeling of heat and bodies surrounding me—a sea of people all one at that very moment. Sophie pulls me closer to her as a guy scoots past and I grin, throwing my hands up in time with the chorus of the music, singing the lyrics as loud as I can. The energy is screaming.

"If somebody had told me I would be seeing this tonight I'd have said they could shove it," a loud voice shouts behind me. I turn around, bumping straight into Evan and his friends as he catches me falling. I wave at Damon and Tom and frown at Evan, stepping out of his reach when I regain my balance.

"What the hell are you doing here?"

"It's nice to see you too." Evan smirks, leaning in to tell me as I can't hear over the music. He looks over my shoulder at Sophie. "You didn't tell her?"

"Forgot." Sophie shrugs.

"Tell me what?"

"Evan called earlier. Wanted to get you out of the house," Sophie explains.

"You're telling me this is his idea?"

"And it has worked," Tom jumps in.

I watch Evan out of the corner of my eye as I hug Damon and Tom properly and see a girl loop her arm over Evan's neck, pulling him to her level and whispering something to him. Something stabs the pit of my stomach and my whole body tells me to look away, but I can't. I see him mutter something back to her and she furrows her eyebrows, tosses a look our way and her eyes land on me.

"You could do better," I can hear her say through the second of quiet music as the DJ changes tracks. It makes me stop breathing. I can feel my insecurities alerting my body and my mind shaking with the possible thoughts she might be thinking. I'm conscious of everything: my body, my hair, my face. It's as if I'm standing naked in front of her and she's got a magnifying glass, scrutinizing every single part of me. Suddenly, this idea doesn't seem fun anymore and I can feel myself curling into the shell I have been living in for weeks now.

"I don't need better," I hear Evan tell her. "I just need her."

I'm not even sure if it is the alcohol or not, I might be drunker than I thought, but the moment is so overwhelming that I stumble back a couple of steps. My mind racing. I stare at Evan, my mind whirling with feelings and thoughts. I suddenly feel so overwhelmed, like I can't really breathe. He shrugs as she walks away and turns back to us like nothing ever happened. I realize he must have palmed off her eagerness and pretended I was his girlfriend or something.

It was just one of those in-the-moment things I tell myself. *Nothing to get yourself worked up about, Kayla.*

But I am worked up about it. It's like I'm feeling every single emotion I have been avoiding addressing for a long time. I feel admiration, respect, trust, *love*. I feel every second we have spent together hit me one at a time. Each memory icing itself into my brain. I look at Evan and I see someone I want to spend time with. I look at Evan and I see someone who I hope wants to spend time with me. And it isn't fate or second chances or any of the Hollywood bullshit movies and soapy romance novels shove into your face to remind you that this is something you'll never have. This is real. This is now. This is love and it's not simple and it's not easy, it's complicated and messy and makes you immerse yourself into it so completely that you don't think you'll ever find a way out.

I'm thoroughly and unconditionally in love with Evan Winters.

But when I look back at my group of friends, this time I don't stumble back just a couple of steps. I almost fall to the floor. My eyes are streaming with something. Not tears, not anger.

Jealousy.

Her arms are tight around his neck and his arms are planted around her waist. Their lips are touching, and his hand has found its way to cup her cheek.

Sophie is kissing Evan.

Evan is kissing Sophie.

And all I want to do is scream.

• • •

Vodka is a load of shit. It does nothing to you as you're drinking it, but the moment you think you're fine, you find yourself in the corner wishing you never existed. I realize eight shots down, grunting my problems to the barman that I am completely overreacting. Despite being balls deep pissed off, I realize that Sophie is neither aware of my feelings towards Evan, and neither is he. I don't have anyone to blame but myself. Sophie hasn't exactly broken the girl code as she hasn't been informed that there is one.

Oh, God. I pull myself from the bar stall and head toward the back door of the club. I can feel the vodka start to work my body as I stumble across the dance floor, bodies crashing into me at all angles. I'm trying so hard to concentrate on getting through that when someone's hand wraps around my arm. I don't peg until I'm forced to turn around and see Evan looking down at me.

"Where have you been?" He leans into me, so I can hear.

"What?" I reply, pulling a face. But it comes out more like 'wot.'

"We have been looking for you for ages." He raises an eyebrow slightly as I start to sway to the music. I almost turn around and say *glad you've noticed between coming up for air with my best friend and shoving your tongue down her throat.*

But I don't say anything. I carry on acting like he doesn't exist.

"How much have you had to drink?" he yells in my ear.

"I am a bird." It's a statement.

He starts to laugh. "And I'm an eagle, but I'm afraid this isn't the Birds of Prey auditorium." Evan licks his lips and presses them together as he pulls away. I've noticed it's something he does when he's impatient. "But I came to find you because Sophie has been sick. Really sick. She's in the girl's restrooms. I'd check on her, but I'm not equipped with a vagina."

I want to laugh, but I'm scared if I do I will be the one doing the puking. For some reason, my mind takes forever to process this information. By the time I can reply, (with what can only be the most stupid thing to do when you're blazing drunk and with hurt feelings) is to tell the person you love, that you love them. But I do.

Of course, I do, because I wouldn't be me if I didn't come out with these types of things in the worst situations ever.

"*I lub you.*" But as I am saying it, Evan's back is turned, and he is walking towards the restrooms. He doesn't hear me.

So, to say I was in a predicament I didn't expect to be in at nine o'clock this morning would have been an understatement. To say the least, it isn't all my fault. I didn't expect to be lining up in a night club's restroom holding back my best friend's hair while she emptied the contents of her binge. I also didn't expect for Evan Winters to be here, raging drunk with his friends and kissing said friend before she was about to puke. But then again, this morning it didn't even occur to me this situation would happen. I was neither in the mood to go out anywhere or expect that I would *ever* feel this stomach punching jealousy in the pit of my stomach over a guy who I had always referred his name with the middle finger to.

But I'm here, blaming myself for drinking too much to think while the beatings of cheap booze already taking effect on my body. I might not have expected this sort of thing to happen at nine o'clock this morning, but then I also didn't think it is possible for me to drunkenly tell Evan Winters I really loved him and him to not even hear over the screams of what this club called their music.

But I did. And it feels absolutely terrible.

Chapter Twenty-Seven

The most aggravating thing about this situation is that neither Evan nor Sophie seem to remember anything. It's like the whole night has washed over their heads and ultimately, it is like it never happened. I try not to be pissed, really—I have no right. Neither of them was aware of my feelings, hell, I didn't until that night. But something cruel stirs in the pit of my stomach every time I think of both of them. Something jealous and unfamiliar. I don't like it and it's making me crazy. I'm not usually a jealous person.

So, I do what any normal person would do: I avoid them.

And it works for almost a week before I have both of them knocking on my front door. I can hear Sophie's voice humming through the letterbox as she impatiently tells me to let her in. I feel myself start to cry standing the other side of the door, my back pressed against the wall and my eyes closed, hoping they will leave. I pray to God that they will go, but it's no use. I know it's not fair to treat them like this. They were both absolutely drunk, it was probably a spur of the moment thing and neither of them meant it, but I can't help feeling betrayed by the two people I care about most in the world. It's like a kick when you're already down.

But avoiding them only lasts so long, and even though the two of them left, the knocking ceased, and the letterbox shut, Evan still found a way to see me. I am woken that night by the window opening. I have resumed my routine of sleeping all day, emailing Adam to see what he is up to and feeling far too emotional to do anything about it. I don't have to turn over to see it's him. I recognize the way his feet plod lightly against my bedroom floor and the way he breathes a sigh of relief for making it. I pretend to be asleep, closing my eyes and lowering my breathing to the level I think a normal person would have when sleeping.

"I know you're not sleeping because I saw you get up just five minutes ago to use the restroom," Evan's voice whispers. The bed dips and I can feel him sitting on the edge, his back turned to me. "Nobody falls asleep that quick, especially you."

"Go away."

"I don't want to," he tells me. It's almost automatic.

"Well, it's my house and I want you to go," I murmur against my pillow, my eyes still shut.

"I don't think you really mean that…" His voice is really quiet, so I don't hear the rest of what he is saying.

"You don't know what I want." I turn, my bed covers falling loosely around my body and face his back. He looks over his shoulder and turns too, sitting crossed legged on my bed.

"I know why you're pissed at us."

Us like Sophie and Evan are something. I ball my fists in my duvet. *Us, us, us.*

"I don't know what you're talking about." I try to sound as sincere as I can, sitting up slightly on my pillow.

"Don't, Kayla." Evan shakes his head. "Don't be stubborn. Just admit it, you're pissed."

"I'm not being stubborn!" I cry, then throw my palm against my lips, worrying I have just woken my mom and my brother. Evan and I look at the door intently, but we don't hear any footsteps.

"I was drunk," he starts. "It didn't mean anything."

"So, you *do* know?" I scoff. "Why would you pretend nothing happened? That just makes it worse." I frown, moving so that I can see his face better, reading his facial expressions. He is wearing a look of genuine confusion, tapping his fingers against his knee.

"I…oh for God's sake, Damon told us yesterday. He said this is likely the reason you've been pissed and avoiding both of us," Evan explains. "I don't remember any of it, and I suppose that's a sign to show it didn't mean anything. If I thought it did, wouldn't I remember doing it?"

"That isn't the point Evan!" I shake my head. "You kissed my best friend. You kissed her, and you threw it in my face."

He looks agitated. "I didn't even know you were there!"

I raise an eyebrow. "That doesn't make sense. You said you don't remember it."

"I don't."

"Then how would you have known if I was there or not?"

"The only thing I remember is grabbing someone, you . . . no . . . *Sophie* . . . and then kissing her. I don't remember who was around, what song was playing, let alone what I was drinking. I'm sorry. I don't understand why this all matters to you so much. That kiss meant nothing to me." Evan's voice softens.

"I can't do this," I say after a short while of silence. I can feel the tears pool in my eyes and I turn away from him, not wanting him to see me cry. "Just go, *please.* Just go."

Evan leans over, touches my knee barely. "I'm never going to just *go.* Not ever. Not really." But he stands up and disappears the same way he came in—without so much as a noise.

• • •

"How are you feeling, Kayla? I don't want fine, or good, I want an answer. How are you feeling?" My therapist sits on my bed.

Since I haven't been going to her, she's been coming to me which I'm not even sure is legal. She's even changed—wearing jeans and a pink V-neck shirt—as if she's my friend and this is a sleepover.

I sit on the opposite side of the bed, still wearing the same nightshirt I've worn for days and shake my head. This is pointless. "Why?"

"Because if you don't talk about it, all that spiraling emotion is going to build and build, and one day it's going to build so much you're going to be carrying a volcano on your back. It only takes one more thing to add fuel to the heat for it to explode. Answer the question, Kayla." Her voice hardens slightly, and she sits up, looking more sincere.

"How am I feeling?" I press my lips together not sure where to start. "I feel as if I am drowning. All I can think about since coming home is about all the people I left behind. The ones I didn't help or the people that I won't ever see again. I think about Adam and how, despite the inevitability that he wasn't forever, he was present. He was the good in the shit situation. He was somebody that wasn't from home but understood everything I was feeling anyway."

"But that isn't it, is it?" She shifts on my bed so that she's facing me properly.

"I don't know how I am supposed to continue living my life when so many people are dead. I don't understand how it's fair for me to get on a plane and leave a city that's in chaos. Call me ridiculous, but I feel like I have abandoned all of those people."

My therapist plays with the hair band on her wrist and looks at me through the strands of her hair that fall over her eyes as she dips her head. "Your problem isn't that you feel you have abandoned them." She therapist hesitates before continuing, "You feel abandoned by everyone else. And it isn't in the literal sense that you weren't with other people, it's the emotional side of you realizing that your life isn't what you thought it was. Ben was your boyfriend, but he hurt you in the most destroying way. He abandoned you in a time that you needed him the most. Our life is built by the pictures we choose to display, and the ones we decide to hide— to keep in the shoebox in our closets—are the ones that need to be aired."

"I feel like I'm not even me anymore," I tell her. "I don't even know if I ever knew who I was." It's the honest truth and it hurts to say it. It means admitting it to myself. I haven't been myself since I was back from Rome. I haven't been able to break out of it either.

"Change is one of the most complex things a human being will ever have to go through. The change within yourself, the shift to a new you will make you rethink everything you have previously known about yourself. Your favorite color, the song you listen to on long drives, the people waiting for you at home. Your change didn't come in a sense where you did the change yourself. Your change came along in a person that the old you hated, the person you thought you could never be friends with. Evan was your change. He did something that not many people have the power to do. He made you feel alive. In the weeks you shared, you didn't have to worry. You didn't realize you were changing because you were too busy being you. But now you're back, now you're here in your old environment, you have no idea what to do with yourself."

Hopeful, I look at her. "So, then what's the answer? What do I do?"

"You see him. You inflict the change into your old environment and make it new. You bring the light into the dark. You light the flame to the fire." She snorts slightly, laughing. "However, you want to put it."

"You can do it." She nods her head reassuringly, almost as if she has read my mind. "And if you can't do it today, you try until you can."

Chapter Twenty-Eight

I don't take her advice.

I don't take it even though every inch of my body tells me to pick up the phone or walk next door. I don't take it when graduation rolls around and Mom ushers me towards the front door wearing a robe and a hat that itches. I don't take it even as I watch him walk on stage and shake the principal's hand, his coffee-colored hair blowing in the breeze and his robe revealing the white shirt he's wearing underneath. I don't take it when I get home and see him packing, the college boxes already piling up in his bedroom, clouding his window with height.

I don't take it when the next week rolls around just as slowly and painfully as the last one had ended. I don't take her advice as I watch Damon and Tom run into Evan's house, armed with cake, coke, and chips and a load of family and friends in tow for his surprise birthday party. I know this because I am invited, not that I responded to the message Damon left me or made an effort to go. I couldn't face seeing him. I don't know how. I can't do it to either of us. I don't want the disappointment. And it's selfish, really selfish.

I don't take her advice because I have no idea what to say. I don't take her advice because there aren't words to say that could justify how I feel, there aren't enough words to make up the months I have spent trying to work them out. I don't take her advice. I don't have to. I don't go to Evan because he comes to me.

•   •   •

Tomorrow I leave for college. Tomorrow I will say goodbye to this bedroom and be traveling to NYU to study medicine. Not my first choice, but my depression meant the hard work I had put into gaining my 4.0 GPA faulted in the last two months before graduation. School had tried to give me some leeway considering the circumstances, but you can't lie to colleges.

Tomorrow I leave, but all I can think about is what I'm leaving behind today. It's late at night and I'm packing away my last necessities I have been keeping out to use. My bedroom is ripped from everything that made it mine, most of the stuff packed away with only some things remaining for when I come back. Mom has been on at me for weeks to leave something behind. I guess she wants to walk in here and feel like I'm still there, that I've never left. I'm so consumed by staring at the four walls of my bedroom that I don't hear him until his feet land on the other side of the window.

"I'm leaving tomorrow," I state, folding a sweatshirt into a bag without turning around. I can feel the heat of his stare on my back and the familiar aftershave he always wears drift into the room. I can feel every ache in my body tell me to turn around and run to him, and it takes just about everything not to.

I have to move on. This is all too ridiculous. We are only friends; we are only ever going to be friends.

"I know," he speaks softly. "Me too."

I gulp down the horrible taste that starts to form in my mouth. "Then why are you here?"

"I want to say goodbye." He takes a step forward and the floorboard creaks under him as he moves. He walks until he is directly behind me, almost touching, but with a big enough gap that we don't. I can feel his hot breath tickle my bare neck and his aftershave is stronger now. I try to ignore it, ice him out and continue packing. It's fucking impossible.

"Bye," I murmur, but it's strained.

"I saw Sophie today," Evan begins slowly, carefully like he is treading on dangerous water. "She says you two are talking again."

"I overreacted."

"You reacted reasonably; it was the two of us that shouldn't have done it." I can feel him watching me fold another piece of clothing and he snakes his arm past my waist and folds another shirt for me. I freeze as his arm brushes my waist and watch him neatly place it on top of all the others.

I don't want his help, I think but I can lie as much as I want to myself, it's still a lie.

"I don't want to get into this," I mutter. "Not now."

"I don't know how to tell you this, so I'm going to say in a way that I've learned. I'm a boat..."

"Evan," and I turn. He's so close and my heart falters in my chest. I feel overwhelmed by just looking at him.

He's gorgeous. God, he's gorgeous. I wish the time I had spent without him in my life meant he got uglier, but he hasn't, somehow, he's more gorgeous than before. I'm not really sure how it's fair or possible. He's wearing the shirt his mom had bought him last week for his birthday. I had watched her give it to him and he fills it out perfectly. He looks down at me, reaching out and touching my shoulder softly. His hand is warm, and his touch sends shivers in all directions, and I have never had the urge more than ever to touch him back, to feel him once more.

"No, just listen." He stops me and cuts off my train of thought. "I'm a boat. I'm equipped with sails, a raft, a wheel and all the other crap that goes along with making a boat sail and I—"

"Where are you going with this?" I interrupt, shaking my head.

"Kayla, what I'm trying to say is that it's not about what can make a boat sail, it's how it can stay afloat. I've spent my whole high school experience pushing my way through the sea of people, drowning more and more each year. I avoid answering questions because I don't have the answers. I don't know what I want to be doing in ten years' time, let alone what I want to do in ten minutes. I hate the fact that I am surrounded by teachers who encourage you to see more of a textbook than the world. And I'm a boat. I'm a boat that's drowning despite having all the right equipment to keep it from doing so. I'm drowning, but when I'm with you, I breathe a little easier, I see a little clearer, and I feel a little more. I don't drown with you, Kayla. I don't drown because I'm already afloat. I don't drown because you're the rock in the empty sea. I don't drown because I am in love with you."

The last few months of emotion all flood in at once and I'm overwhelmed by what he is saying that I forget he wants an answer. I think about how every part of how I feel for him is how he feels too and I close my eyes, both wishing the moment will end and last forever all at the same time. His hand drops from my shoulder and I think about my plan.

I can't do this. Not now, it wouldn't be fair. I'm a mess. I've been a mess since I got back months ago. He doesn't want this Kayla, not a girl who is depressed and damaged.

"Evan," I begin and open my eyes, my voice strained.

"Don't." He shakes his head and steps away. "Don't say it because I don't dare think I can take it."

And just like that, I have to pretend I don't feel the same. That this whole thing between us is what we originally planned it to be—something to spark jealously from the two people who toyed with our emotions for too long. But even as I stand here, looking at him, I realize I am no better. For I am too is toying with his emotions like they are nothing.

"I promised I would never fall in love with you," I tell him because it's the only thing I can justify in that moment. "I made a promise to you and to myself."

Evan's lips part and he doesn't hide how much it hurts him. "Kayla, you cannot seriously think that meant something. It was just a joke, a comment."

"I wish it could be different," I whisper.

Evan is silent for a long time and he's so close, in touching distance and I want to reach out to him and ball my face into his chest. I want to feel his arms around me, his lips on mine, and our bodies together.

He takes a step back and I can't feel him anymore. "But we can't always get what we wish for, right?" he replies.

"No." I shake my head slowly and look towards the floor. "We can't."

And I don't know how long we both stand there, in silence. I can hear my heart screaming at me for lying and my eyes are sore from pushing down the tears. I can feel the whole room become an island, one in which I can't escape.

"Goodbye, Kayla," he finally says. But when I dare to look back up, he's already gone.

Chapter Twenty-Nine

Evan

A year later

I don't really like Thanksgiving. I've always thought it as people's way of celebrating Christmas early because people are just impatient. They want the food, the celebration, in some cases, like my family, the gifts. When everything crappy in their life can be celebrated through a holiday. But even so, I find myself in my car driving forty hours towards Los Angeles from my apartment near Columbia University where I have been going to school for the last year. Studying business is something that took me by surprise. The course jumped out at me, the school is perfect and the very first day made me think I could really have a future for the first time. I think about myself ten years from now and can actually *see* something.

One of Justin Bieber's new songs comes on the radio and I find myself reaching over and turning the song up, the tune has been a guilty pleasure of mine for weeks and I'm not ashamed to admit it. I roll to a stop, drumming my fingers to the beat of the music on the steering wheel and look to my left, the sign welcoming me to Los Angeles less than a meter away.

I can't help but think about the last time I was here. It must have been Christmas break, but I wasn't around the house long. Mom has been struggling since her dad passed away and, in all honesty, I haven't been that upset. I just didn't know the guy enough to be devastated by his loss. The sad truth is that Granddad was a man who sent a cheque every birthday and Christmas. He wasn't somebody our family saw on the regular. So maybe it was due to the fact I wasn't emotionally tethered to my granddad in ways other people are, or the fact I have had more than I can handle with people trampling on my heart, that I've kind of just shut it off, pretended that my heart doesn't exist.

It takes me almost forty-five minutes to get past all the Hollywood stuff and into the outer boroughs of L.A and to my street. I'm surprised as I drive down that everything still looks exactly the same, a year on. I didn't know exactly what I expected, of course, it would look the same. Noticeable change never occurs in that short of a time, or at least nothing people really notice.

I drive past the old church Mom had dragged my younger sister and me to every Sunday before she realized that none of our family were much believers in God or anything else spiritual. I think she thought taking us would mean she was carrying something on from her own upbringing.

It's the kind of hot today that makes me sweat in places I really wish I wouldn't. I guess I never appreciated LA weather until moving to college. It is one of the one things I miss about being at home. I roll down the window to get more air as the air con doesn't do much in the old truck I've driven for years.

The further I drive down the street, the closer I am to *her* house. It stands like everyone else's on this street, the same front yard with her mom's car parked outside. I notice because I'm looking for hers, which isn't there. She must not be back yet. I'm not about to lie and say it doesn't make me feel relieved that I have beat her to it, no awkward encounter. It means we can continue to ignore each other and pretend like the last time I'd talked to her, she didn't stamp over my heart and throw it out of the window.

I pull up to my driveway and Mom's already out of the door before I can cut the engine.

"You've gotten taller," she says and hugs me before I'm even properly out of the door.

"No," I say. "Still the same." And close my car door behind me.

Mom pulls away and frowns. "Well, something's changed,"

"You say that every time you see me." I shake my head, chuckling. It's true.

"Because I never see you." She pouts her bottom lip. "Something's always changing." She spins around and faces the dozens of boxes she has lined up next to the garage. "On the topic of change, I am renovating the garage."

"You are?" I look over her shoulder and see the garage empty, the flooring pulled up and two men working on the ceiling. I'm surprised I hadn't noticed as I drove up, but I know my attention is never on my own house.

"Yeah, I am going to make it a space for Chelsea," she tells me referring to my younger sister. As if on cue, Chelsea herself turns up at the front door, someone behind her. She sees me with Mom and runs over, her arms around my waist before I can blink. I hug her back and smile. I've missed her.

"I've missed you, munchkin," I tell her, kissing the top of her forehead.

"And you." she smiles back at me. "Did Mom tell you about the garage?"

"Yeah. Cool, huh?"

"Cameron loves it." She nods, beckoning over her shoulder. I see Kayla's younger brother in the doorway awkwardly waiting for Chelsea to return to whatever they were playing. I said a year doesn't change much, but Cameron is already staggering over five foot and seems to have grown up too much since I last saw him. They're only ten. He looks exactly like Kayla, same brown hair and eyes. His mom's thin lips though. Kayla always had fuller lips.

I shake out my thoughts of Kayla and look down at Chelsea. "Of course, he does. It's gonna be awesome!"

"He says his sister's in town." And despite Chelsea's young age, she's always been undoubtedly perceptive. I think she's always known.

"Did he? I didn't see her car as I pulled up," I say slowly, casually... *normally.*

"I think she went out a while ago." Chelsea shrugs.

"Right."

"Oh, and Mom said she found this when clearing out, made me promise not to open it because it wasn't addressed to me." Chelsea hands me a folded piece of paper with my name scribbled on the top of it. I take it from her and ruffle her hair, leaving the front porch and going into the house. I make my way to my bedroom, flopping down on my bed, the note tossed on my pillow. I'll read it later.

It's almost an hour later before I remember to read it. Unpacked and showered, I see the paper on my pillow and sit down on the edge of my bed, a towel around my waist. I heard someone's car rattle up the driveway over twenty minutes ago and presume Kayla was back from wherever she had been. It sounds pathetic, but since then, I've avoided looking out the window that mirrors hers. I don't want to accidentally see her.

The piece of paper is bent slightly and looks as if someone has screwed it up and then changed their mind afterward. I open it, regardless, my nose wrinkling as the letter starts off.

I thought that the night in the club was the day I realized I was in love with you. I thought between the people dancing and the alcohol racing through every vein in my body that this moment here is the moment I have decided I'm in love with you, Evan Winters. But it wasn't. That was the moment I had admitted it to myself. The moment I decided I was in love with you wasn't when you were planning to ensure that the sixty-odd students and teachers survived, or when we were running from the Italian police with a dozen chickens. It was the moment where nothing was happening at all. When one night in that safe haven hotel I had to get up for a glass of water and I saw you. You were sleeping, and it was late. The room was dark and the feeling was so extraordinary I had pushed it to the back of my mind. It was then that I knew that whether I wanted to or not, I was completely in love with you. And the most frustrating part of loving someone is knowing that you can't do anything about it to make it stop. And that's what I wanted. To make it stop. I knew that loving you was a one-sided ordeal, that nothing good could come out of it.

But our life isn't a movie. I'm not stuck in a Nicholas Sparks book where everything goes the way you want it to. This is real, and this is now.

So, I'm not sure if when reading this, you'll remember the boat analogy you told me. If you don't, I didn't say anything because I too hate giving answers to questions that I don't know how to reply to. But here it goes: you said I was the rock in your empty sea, the one that kept you afloat. But it was you who spent your time making sure I wouldn't drown. It was you who made me stay afloat.

I won't tell you what it's like to love someone like you because describing it would be the single easiest and hardest thing I'll ever have to do. So instead, I'll give you this: You gave me a view on life that nobody had ever bothered to share. You taught me what it was like to forgive, laugh, cry, and care all the same time. You gave me moments in the days I needed the most.

Okay, I think I've figured it out and you're gonna have to bear with me on this one. Loving you is like being alone in a dark part of town, looking over your shoulder, folding your arms in. It is like exhaling the smell of honeycomb and running my tongue against your liquor stained lips. It feels as if I am standing on the back of your moped hair, shirt flying. You are the metaphor for intoxicating, and you are completely and utterly exhilarating.

So…if by some chance, you get this then let me tell you I am sorry for leaving you like I did. I thought by stepping back you would have a chance to get over this blip. This moment. This wasn't supposed to happen—this love. But it did. And I'm glad. I'll always be glad.

Yours,

Kayla

Like she had been watching the whole time, my gaze lifts from the piece of crumpled paper and to the window. I see her in her bedroom. Her hair is pulled back into a bun and she's wearing a shirt that reads *FOREVER OR NOW* and I'm not sure whether it's coincidental or funny. The paper still glued to my fingertips, I stand, walking towards the window. She's standing there, her perfect bundle of beauty and clumsiness all meshed into one. She's not smiling, she doesn't have too. Her eyes latch onto the piece of paper in my hand. She takes a slow step back and suddenly I can't see her anymore.

"Oh, fuck it," I mutter to myself, pulling on a shirt and pair of shorts and open the window I have climbed out of too many times. I struggle to climb across the tree I have spent my life climbing and tug at her window at the opposite side. I still can't see her as I slip in, always knocking my foot against the window sill and plodding slowly into her bedroom. It looks exactly how she left it. Exactly like Kayla.

"What are you doing here?" her voice comes from the other side of the room, hovering near the bathroom door.

"Why didn't you tell me?" I whisper, holding the letter out to her. "Why write it down?"

"I didn't know how to tell you. I didn't think I ever could," her reply is almost automatic, as if she's thought about this. The more I think about this, the more my heart pulls. She's thought about this moment, she's thought about me, about *us.*

She takes a step forward and I can see she's been crying.

"It hasn't changed, and I know I'm probably so late, but I have spent a year trying my hardest to get over you, to stop this love and this insane amount of hope that you would ever feel remotely the same back to me again. Seeing you now makes it so much harder because you're so freaking perfect and so fucking familiar." She gulps and walks the short distance between us. Her hand reaches my chest, just below my heart. "I did the worst thing anyone can do: I let you go. And it was the hardest thing I have ever had to do, but considering you're here, I am hoping that we can at least be frie—"

But her words are interrupted by my lips and it feels a thousand times better than I have ever imagined—a whole lot more magical than I would give Nicholas Sparks or whoever she always quotes credit for. I move my hands so that they run through her hair, tracing circles down her back until I get to her waist. I can feel her own hands slip under my t-shirt, the warmth from her fingertips on my back. The moment isn't perfect, our kissing is breathless and overdue, but it doesn't matter that the moment isn't perfect. It doesn't need to be. It is ours…and that's all that matters.

THE END

Can't get enough of Kayla and Evan? Make sure you sign up for the author's blog to find out more about them!

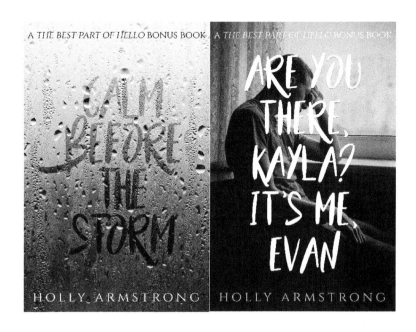

Get these two bonus chapters and more freebies when you sign up at hollie-armstrong.awesomeauthors.org!

Here is a sample from another story you may enjoy:

FROM THE AUTHOR THAT BROUGHT YOU
THE BEST FRIEND

The *Tweet*

ALLY WILLIAMS

Chapter 1

A Ding Changed Everything

Odeya

Some may consider me clinically insane, which is fine; they just don't get it.

I simply think I'm slightly obsessed with a certain European singer who doesn't know I exist.

Sad when it's put that way, I know.

I'm not quite sure when I fell down the dark rabbit hole of one unrealistic, Greek god, but I fucking tumbled in without a regret. Well, all but one. My wallet isn't exactly the happiest with me.

Needless to say, my wondering thoughts have distracted me from the history homework I was supposed to complete hours ago. But who can blame me? What kind of monster assigns any type of school work on a Friday?

It's hard enough to focus any other day, but one that's considered a weekend might as well be a crime. Fortunately, I can see the end of senior year like a bright light of hope at the end of this dark tunnel. So, it's too late to drop out now.

It's a mystery how I've managed four years of high school alongside brain-dead peers without slamming my head so hard into a wall that I bleed to death.

I've considered it; trust me.

Deciding that I've had enough torture for one night, I scoff and slam the unnaturally heavy history book shut. I stand from the rock-hard chair with my laptop in hand. I flop myself down on the bed instead, shuffling further up to sink into the comfy duvet.

As soon as the screen powers up and my tanned face is lit, I log into Twitter. Almost immediately, my feed is full of people losing their shit. I scroll up and down; it's the same thing for hours on end.

And this is what I get for doing my homework.

There is a lot of gibberish, but I manage to pull a few coherent words here and there. Turns out Theo had his newest song—that he's been teasing—leaked.

One of two things must have happened here: a brainiac fan managed to put it out there, or he leaked it himself. Either way, I'm not surprised.

My integrity is on the line. My fingers are itching to click the link to hear the beautiful melodies, but I also want to be loyal. This is *his* life. We should at least have the respect to wait and listen when he want us to.

Going with my gut and better judgement, I move the mouse to the red circle to close the tab instead. Waiting will make it even better. That's what I'm telling myself, at least. I'll just have to avoid social media at all costs.

"They're trying to kill me." I sigh in distress, overdramatically falling against my pillows.

I don't judge people just by their looks; however, one person with shining grey eyes and tousled brown locks caught my eye—Theo Ashford.

I can't explain why he drew me in the second I saw his face, but he did. It was this undeniable attraction that I felt growing in the pit of my stomach, and he has managed to hold my heart ever since.

Now I definitely sound clinically insane.

I'm aware that he'll never know of my existence, and I don't truly know him. I've never been to any of his concerts or live television shows, nor have I ever ran into him at the grocery store. My luck isn't good like that. But I'd like to think that he is pretty true to how he conveys himself on camera.

Sadly enough, I've been a fan since the start. Though the past two years have become strenuous, knowing I won't be able to meet the guy who has single-handedly put a smile on my face after having an anxiety attack.

Should I just give it all up? Distance myself and stop overly obsessing? Support at an arm's length? Or continue and let the sadness grow over the fact that I can't ever know him? It has been a constant tug of war in my brain.

In the four years that I've followed him through everything, I've never once reached out to him via any form. I know that he would never see it. My luck sucks, so I'd just be wasting my time. He's out there dating models while I'm just a fangirl who's still in high school, sitting at home on a Friday night, looking at pictures of him like a long-lost lover.

Why not switch it up a bit? It's not like he will ever see it out of the million messages he gets. So, why not?

@OdeyaBello: @TheoAshford If I'm being honest, you're truly fucking up my life...

I huff and roll my eyes. Why do I let a single boy have so much control over my life when he doesn't even know me? Hell, when I don't even personally know him! Maybe it's about time that I move on with my life.

As sad as that thought is, I am growing up. High school is almost done, and I'll be going to college, hopefully, so I can't let my life revolve around a guy. It's getting a bit out of hand.

Taking a break from the internet—which is pathetic since I've only been logged on for a minute—I slide off my mattress and advance towards my bedroom door to grab a snack downstairs.

Right as my fingers grip the knob, my computer dings loudly. I stop in my tracks and slowly turn my head as if I were in a horror movie.

I trudge hesitantly back to my previous spot, anxiously sitting on the edge of my bed. It may just be one of my oh-so-supportive friends telling me to stop stalking a famous guy.

I was wrong. So wrong.

@TheoAshford: @OdeyaBello How so, love? X

If you enjoyed this sample then look for
<u>The Tweet</u>

Other books you might enjoy:

Playing The Field
Kay SH

Available on Amazon!

Other books you might enjoy:

Saving Gracie
Talesha Mitchell

Available on Amazon!

Acknowledgements

To all my lovely readers who have supported me on not just one, not two, but three different drafts of this book. Thank you all for loving Kayla and Evan as much as I do.

Author's Note

Hey there!

Thank you so much for reading The Best Part Of Hello! I can't express how grateful I am for reading something that was once just a thought inside my head.

I'd love to hear from you! Please feel free to email me at hollie_armstrong@awesomeauthors.org and sign up at hollie-armstrong.awesomeauthors.org for freebies!

One last thing: I'd love to hear your thoughts on the book. Please leave a review on Amazon or Goodreads because I just love reading your comments and getting to know YOU!

Whether that review is good or bad, I'd still love to hear it!

Can't wait to hear from you!

Hollie Armstrong

About the Author

Nineteen-year-old (self) proclaimed mess of bad hair days and under eye circles. Hollie Armstrong is usually found with her head in a book or on her laptop, but when she's not doing that, she enjoys just about everything else!

At the moment she is enjoying a gap year before starting university where she plans to spend ten weeks at a summer camp in the US as a camp counselor.

She has been writing seriously since the passing of her Grandpa who was her inspiration and supporter since day one. She completed her first book in December 2015 and has finished an additional two since that time.